H2S,
HOME SWEET HOME

NICHOLAS SNOW

Translation by
Helen Politis & Vicki Politis

Table of Contents

CHAPTER I

Bombing

Squadron Leader Robert Rodger's gaze was fixed on the display of the H2S radar apparatus, virtually the only source of light in the Lancaster's cockpit.[1] As the navigator/radar operator of the aircraft, he was seated under the dome of the cockpit next to the navigator, behind the pilot and the flight engineer who also functioned as co-pilot. The dome gave him a clear view of the night sky, allowing them to navigate by the stars as well, just as in the early days of the war. Opposite them sat the wireless operator. The Lancaster's manufacturers had designed the cockpit so as to allow all crewmembers seated there the best possible visibility in all directions.

By December 1943, all this was history.

---

[1]   Avro Lancaster: The top four-engine bomber of the Royal Air Force. Normally carrying a seven-man crew, it frequently carried an eighth man as in the case of the Pathfinder Squadron which added a navigator/radar operator. The maximum payload was 14,000lbs though in 1945, specially modified Lancasters carried the largest bomb of the war, the 20,000lbs Grand Slam.

Mechanical aids and electronic eyes had taken over navigation, transforming the navigators who up to that point differed little from their predecessors, the great explorers of the Renaissance, into technocrats of a new age. Progress was swift. Both the Luftwaffe, when it began its night raids on London in September 1940, as well as the RAF when it counter-attacked, quickly realized that even though the night protected the bombers from enemy fighters, it also rendered them blind, unable not only to spot specific targets but even entire cities – and even more so the further afield the cities targeted were from home base.

Enter the age of electronic navigation, first with the GEE and then the OBOE systems of the RAF, which guided the bombers with radio signals over the darkened landscape of wartime Europe. These systems functioned by broadcasting synchronized radio signals from ground stations along the English coast directly to the aircraft, pinpointing with relative accuracy the trajectory of the craft as it approached, first, the cities of the Ruhr, and then…

The real revolution soon followed, the development of the cavity magnetron, an invention which allowed radar to be reduced to a size small enough to be carried aboard an aircraft. The giant steel radar towers of the Battle of Britain now seemed as prehistoric as dinosaurs. The cavity magnetron led to the development of the first ground-scanning radar, the H2S. With it, navigators could now see on their displays the characteristics of the surfaces over which they were flying: flatlands, elevations, sea, lakes and rivers – and population centers.

The first fully successful major mission by the RAF that was guided by the initial Mark I model of the H2S system was disastrous for Germany.

The target chosen for that mission was intentionally an easy one: the precision of the image produced using 10cm wavelengths proved sufficient to form an excellent electronic map of Hamburg, thanks to the city's location at the confluence of the sea and the Elbe River. On the night of July 24, 1943, Operation Gomorrah began, reaching its climax three days later. Seven hundred and twenty-nine bombers struck the city with 2,326 tons of explosive and incendiary bombs.

The result? "The devastation was catastrophic", as the city's Chief of Police wrote. Hellfire devoured the city, just as it had biblical Gomorrah.

And, after Hamburg, came the turn of the biggest prize of all for the RAF, the target of all targets: Berlin, the heart of the Reich, the source of evil, a city of 3.3 million inhabitants and a surface area of 883 square miles.

The first raid on the night of November 18 was disappointing: the image of the city on the radar displays was not clearly definable because, in contrast to Hamburg, the landscape of Brandenburg was not favourable: there was no sea, no mountain, not even a river like the Elbe, just one monotonous, flat surface with many lakes, large and small, as well as little rivers that only served to confuse even the most experienced radar operators. The darker patches and lines in the image were water surfaces, but which of these lines was the Spree River, which lakes or ponds were they actually seeing? The lighter patches were land surfaces, but what exactly were they? Fields, hills, more fields full of even lighter patches indicating villages, towns, cities, the outskirts of Berlin, its centre, what exactly?

There were many, and their numbers kept increasing, who felt that the RAF's operations were costing the nation too many aircraft, too much money and too many lives, without results. The programme of the Bomber Command was absorbing almost 50% of Great Britain's spending on defence, with the promise that it would cripple the production capacity of the Third Reich and break the morale of the German people.

The results of the series of raids on Berlin that began on the night of November 18 with hundreds of four-engine bombers were unsatisfactory. Reconnaissance flights by swift Mosquitoes, flying high during daylight to escape enemy fighters, revealed that the dispersion of the bombs was too great. Only one bomb in three had landed within the greater Berlin area and only one in six had hit the centre of the city. The H2S MkI in this instance was not up to the task of providing bombing accuracy.

On this night, December 29, all this would change, thanks to the latest version of the H2S, the Mark III, and Rodger himself would be instrumental in that change.

The MkIII version, in contrast with the MkI which produced 10cm wavelengths, produced 3cm wavelengths, with the result that the beam of the radar's signal was narrower, more focused, displaying the landscape with greater accuracy. This was proven in trials over Great Britain: small lakes that on the old system appeared as one were now clearly discernible as two.

Rodger stared at the display as the radar's beam scanned the landscape below from the aerial housed in the radome under the fuselage of the Lancaster. They were nearing Berlin.

'Three degrees correction to the left,' he instructed the Lancaster's pilot, S.J. Ireland over the intercom. 'Steady now...'

He was certain that what he was seeing now on the display was the outline of the Spree River. It was so clear, it was as if he was seeing it in broad daylight with a naked eye, exactly matching the image burned into his mind after studying aerial photographs and maps for endless hours. He knew there was no need to consult the map laid out on the table in front of him.

'Can you make out the river below?' Rodger asked, speaking into the VHF radio connecting him to the navigators of the two other Pathfinder Lancasters[2] also equipped with the new radar.

'Copy!' came back the voice of one of them.

'Copy!' he heard the other respond.

'It's the Spree, leading us into the heart of the city.'

Rodger spoke again over the intercom to his pilot, adjusting course for a bend in the river. 'Shift slightly to the right...a little more...now steady...steady...a little more...we're almost there...'

Suddenly the night sky ahead burst into light as the city's air defence forces kicked into action. Giant searchlights lit up the landscape as their beams shot up into the blackness of the night sky,

---

[2]   Pathfinder: The special RAF bomber squadron whose Lancasters led the raids, marking the target either with flares or incendiary bombs. The crews were the most experienced and the aircraft were equipped with the most sophisticated electronics.

long, brilliant fingers, narrow at the source then gradually splaying out as they shifted about, searching, trying to snare an enemy aircraft for the anti-aircraft gunners.

The anti-aircraft batteries began to fire, the first salvos probing, seeking the altitude of the British bombers. The heavier guns were equipped with radar, but it was not accurate enough. The fate of the bombers hovered between salvation and destruction by a matter of just a few hundred feet off in the accuracy of the AA fire.

The night was alight from the explosions of the AA shells, bright flashes, some far off, others nearer, a rainstorm of angry harbingers. The force of some of the closer shell bursts rocked the aircraft, like a sudden gust of wind tossing a leaf about in the air. The sound of the explosions reached the aircraft like a muffled *swoosh!*, like the rumbling of some mysterious beast of the heavens exhaling.

The pilot had both hands on the controls, constantly adjusting his course as each nearby explosion caused the Lancaster's altitude to dip for a few seconds.

Rodger could not see what lay ahead of the aircraft as the radar display only showed the lower part of the front view. His gaze was fixed on his display.

He centred the beam of the aerial straight ahead. He was certain that what he was seeing ten miles out was the centre of Berlin. He had no doubts: he could see the two dark arms of the river, the one meandering like a snake, the other straighter, as the Spree split in two to embrace the heart of the city, the great park with its zoo, a flat, open expanse of land that appeared lighter on his display between the river's arms. Around it, even lighter, the built-up areas of the city.

In confirmation, Rodger made out the outline of the tiny lake Neuer Zee and the creek that led out of it through the length of the park.

A nearby explosion rocked the Lancaster. Rodger barely noticed, engrossed as he was, fascinated by what he was seeing on his display.

'Can you see the fork in the Spree? The Zoo's park? The dark spot in the front is the Neuer Zee, do you see it?'

'Copy!' both the other navigators responded almost simultaneously.

'That's the point of release,' he said, 'the little lake.'

A few seconds more.

'Steady…steady,' he muttered over the intercom to the pilot, feeling each second like a heartbeat.

'Bombardier, ready?'

'Ready! Bomb bay open!'

Rodger knew that the bombardier in the glass bubble under the nose of the Lancaster was focused on his bombsight. He doubted though that even now, over the very centre of the city, if he could make out anything in the dark.

He didn't have to. The H2S would do it for him.

'Now!' Rodger shouted excitedly into both the intercom and the VHS.

The bombardier released the bombs. Almost simultaneously, the other two Pathfinders followed suit.

A new tactic for marking the target was being tested this night. Instead of parachuted flares hovering over the target that tended to be swept away by prevailing winds, the Pathfinders dropped incendiary bombs in the form of canisters that each contained either 236 4-pound phosphorus bombs or 24 36-pounders.

The glow from the fires below that would result would provide the bombardiers of the scores of Lancasters behind them with their target.

'Let's head home!' Rodger cried out to his pilot.

The Lancaster circled wide over the city and set a homeward course, always under the guidance of the H2S system.

Hundreds of four-engine Lancaster, Halifax and Sterling bombers dropped their loads, all aiming at the bright targets marked by the flames of the fires that those first incendiaries had lit.

The Messerschmitt Bf-110 G-4 of *Oberleutnant* Heinz Wolfgang Schnaufer, *StaffelKapitän* 12/NJG1[3] had taken off over an hour earlier from its airbase in St. Trond in Holland.

The German Würzburg ground radar system had been blinded by the use of Window[4] by the British bombers, 27cm long, 2cm wide aluminium strips that were dropped by the thousands, each half the length of the wavelength of the German radar. This blinded the radar, allowing the bombers to pass unobserved.

But now, Schnaufer and the other German fighter pilots had been informed that the British target for that night's raid had been Berlin,

---

[3]   *Staffelkapitän*: Commander of a Luftwaffe squadron which consisted of 12 aircraft. 12/NJG1 or, *Nacht Jagdgeschwader*, indicated the 12th squadron of Night Fighter Wing 1. Schnaufer, then an *Oberleutnant*, survived the war with the rank of major, the ace of aces of the German Night Fighter command with 121 victories. The vertical stabilizer of the last plane he flew is on display at the Imperial War Museum in Lambeth in South London. The fighter's call signal was G9 E2.

[4]   Window: The precursor of today's electronic chaff radar countermeasure.

which had just been hit. The bombers were on their way back home and Schnaufer and his pilots were able to estimate roughly the course they would take out of Europe, over the Channel and back to their bases in England.

'Heinz, ground control notes interference,' his *Bordfunker*[5] informed him. 'At coordinates…'

The operator gave him the coordinates and Schnaufer adjusted his course accordingly. Interference meant that Window had been dropped to provide cover for the returning bombers.

Ground radar could not locate the bombers because of the interference but if they got close enough, with a little luck, they might spot one of them with the help of their plane's radar.

Schnaufer had faith in his wireless operator, in the FuG 202[6] radar, in his own cat-like night vision and in their luck - and not necessarily in that order. And be that as it may, even on a very dark night such as this, it wasn't easy for several hundred four-engine bombers to slip by unnoticed.

'Heinz, we're getting close to the area of interference. I'm activating the radar,' Schnaufer's wireless operator said over the intercom.

Schnaufer scanned the night sky all around him.

Nothing.

Darkness below, starry sky high above. No dark shadow that might indicate enemy bombers.

---

[5]   *Bordfunker*: Wireless and radar operator

[6]   FuG: literally this was an acronym for "radio equipment" (*FunkGerät*) but referred to all onboard electronics, including, as in this case, the airborne radar apparatus.

The fighter, painted pale blue, with grey camouflage markings on its upper surfaces, with its long fuselage and its round snout, resembled a shark swimming in the night sky searching for its prey, the herd of bombers.

Schnaufer waited silently for his wireless operator to speak, tension flooding through his body. His felt an itch in his left palm suddenly. He felt an urge to scratch hard, painfully. For a few seconds he clasped the controls between his knees and scratched his palm.

He was sure of it. The itch was a warning from his built-in radar that the bombers were nearby.

'Willy, still nothing?' he asked, needlessly, just to break the tension a little by hearing the sound of his own voice.

Willy was focused on his display. According to ground control, they were now flying in the area of the interference. He briefly activated the Naxos system[7], searching for emissions from the British H2S radar. When these were detected by the system all he had to do then was guide his pilot toward their source, the enemy bomber.

Nothing. The Naxos remained blind and mute. No indication…. How was this possible? Didn't the British have to use their radar to find their way home? Or had ground control made a mistake, leading them astray, the bombers now out of Naxos' range?

Willy activated the radar again, its signal radiating from the four antennae extending out of the fighter's nose. With his eyes glued to the display, he waited to spot a bounce off some object, an object that could only be an enemy plane…

---

[7]   FuG 350 Naxos Z: essentially, a receiver of the 10cm wavelength emissions of the H2S MKI, not however, of the 3cm of the MKIII.

Schnaufer played a little with his foot pedals controlling his tail wings rudder, adjusting his course slightly to increase the area scanned by his radar's beam.

Willy suddenly noticed an almost imperceptible blip at the edge of his display which vanished almost immediately as the fighter changed course.

'Heinz, shift to the right 8-10 degrees!' he cried out, agitated.

As soon as the Messerschmitt adjusted course, the blip showed up on Willy's display again, first at the edge then moving toward its centre.

'*Emil! Emil!*'[8] Willy yelled excitedly.

The trace was some 7,000 feet away and Willy, eyes focused on his display, began to guide Schnaufer toward their target.

Schnaufer opened the throttles of his two engines, quickly picking up speed. Within seconds he reached top speed, some 300 miles per hour. Now he could feel the vibrations of the engines and even, in spite of his earphones, hear their monotone buzz, sounding like a growl.

'Six thousand feet, altitude 300,' Willy intoned. 'Three degrees right…steady now…slight shift to the left…steady…5000 feet…altitude still 300…steady…can you see him?…4500…steady, 4000…he's changing course…correct, five degrees right…same altitude…3500 feet…'

Schnaufer's eyes searched the night sky, feeling the every beat of his heart down to his very fingertips. Where the hell was that bomber?

Darkness, stars…hey, wait a minute, why couldn't he see any stars in that patch up there? Immediately, he realized that a

---

8   *Emil, Emil*: the codeword for radar contact.

shadow, a black silhouette was hiding that part of the sky, straight ahead and some 300 feet above him. A shadow that had the shape of a bomber.

'*Ich berühre!*'[9] He whispered into the intercom, as if he feared his voice could be heard, betraying their presence to the bomber's crew who were themselves scanning the skies for their enemy.

His position behind and beneath allowed him the advantage of being difficult to be discerned against the dark background of the earth below while he on the other hand could clearly see the aircraft silhouetted against the paler night sky.

Schnaufer throttled back to almost match the speed of the bomber for his approach, trying to remain in the Lancaster's blind spot without losing sight of it. The fighter slowly gained ground, like a wild beast creeping unnoticed toward its prey. Just a little closer…a little closer… The Lancaster was now above the Messerschmitt, approximately 200 feet higher. If it had been daylight, he would have been flying in its shadow. Schnaufer glanced quickly at his scope, saw the Lancaster's wings extending beyond it, made one last adjustment with his controls and his foot pedals…

Now!

He pushed the button that fired the two 20mm cannon of the *Schräge Musik*.[10] His aircraft shuddered slightly from the recoil as

---

[9]   *Ich berühre*: codeword for visual contact.

[10]   *Schräge Musik*: "weird music". A set of two 20mm cannon set at the rear of the cockpit of the Bf-110 or the fuselage of the Ju-88 aiming upwards at a 70-80 degree angle towards the underbelly of an enemy bomber. It proved to be especially effective.

the cannons fired dozens of bullets at the Lancaster's underbelly. Schnaufer didn't use tracer bullets because he felt they affected his night vision even if it was for just a few seconds. In any event, given his proximity to his target before commencing firing, he could see it so clearly that tracers were not necessary.

Schnaufer and Willy (who now no longer needed to look at his radar display) could see the bright flashes where the bullets aimed decisively by Schnaufer ripped into the Lancaster's most vulnerable spot, the fuel tanks between the inside engine and the point where the wing was attached to the fuselage.

Almost immediately flames flew out, lighting up the sky and the black underbelly of the Lancaster, making it seem so close that they could almost touch it. Willy could clearly make out the large shape of the radome behind the bomb bay doors…so why then hadn't the Naxos picked up anything?

Schnaufer turned the fighter sharply into a shallow dive to escape shrapnel in the event that the tanks on the bomber exploded.

On the Lancaster, the crew's first inkling of the attack was the violent shudder of the aircraft as the bullets struck the wing. The aircraft was suddenly jolted, as if a sudden, powerful gust of wind from below had thrust it upwards, as if some invisible giant hand had slapped it like a plaything upwards a few feet. The pilot lost control of his joystick for a few seconds before grabbing hold of it and struggling to regain control of the aircraft.

The table with the maps in front of Rodger was jarred and his open map flew off, down into the darkness of the plane's interior.

Ireland and the flight engineer looked out. They could see the tail of flames streaming out of the wing's base. Both right engines had stopped. They were quickly losing altitude. Ireland still had control of the Lancaster, but not for much longer. He realized the hit was lethal. Any second the wing could shear off and the plane would fall out of control into a spiral dive or the tanks could blow.

'Bail out!' he ordered his crew, holding on to the controls with all his strength as the Lancaster bucked and jerked as if crashing into airborne obstacles. He had to keep the aircraft steady long enough for his men to bail out.

Rodger, doubled over, followed the wireless operator into the dark interior of the plane, bracing with his hands against the bulkheads to steady himself. The few feet in that darkness seemed to last forever. He made it to the open door on the right side of the fuselage, just a few feet from the tail.

The wireless operator jumped into the void.

Rodger was right behind. He felt the powerful wind at the door, hesitating for a heartbeat.

'Go!' the rear gunner shouted at him.

Rodger jumped out into the void as well.

It was strange, the sudden, absolute silence, the disorientation in the darkness, a sense of freedom, peace, as he had felt when, as a boy, he used to jump off the high rocks into the sea.

Snapping back to reality, he pulled the ripcord, releasing the parachute. He felt the sudden jerk as the parachute unfurled above him, leaving him suspended by the straps, feet aiming at the ground.

Looking up, he could make out the Lancaster like a streaking comet, rapidly losing altitude in the distance.

His parachute, like some supernatural celestial jellyfish above him, slowly brought him down closer and closer to the dark, threatening earth below.

CHAPTER II

Falling

Adolph Gluntz was proud of three things: he bore the same first name as the *Führer*, he wore the uniform of the *Hitlerjügend* and its local leader always had praise for his reports: 'As good as if written by an officer of the Wehrmacht!'

Adolph wasn't thinking about the day ahead, dawning slowly into a dreary cloud-covered sky, a precursor of coming rain, or even snow. Tomorrow was the last day of the year and they would be celebrating the coming of the New Year with the few extra bits of food that could be scrounged up to break the monotony of the ration card. His mother might, no, would certainly bake a strudel, even if it was to be made with that awful ersatz sugar. His father would certainly have saved a nice piece of pork from the last pig he had slaughtered for his mother to prepare with the traditional sauerkraut and boiled potatoes.

No, his thoughts were centred on reaching as soon as possible the English bomber they had seen during the night falling like a flaming comet over the village before it crashed with a deafening explosion. He spotted it a little later in a field about three kilometres from the village.[11]

He quickened his pace and approached the wreckage. One wing with its two engines had broken off the fuselage completely and lay some 50 metres away from the rest of the plane. From models they had been shown and from a previous bomber crash, Adolph recognised it as a Lancaster.

He looked around quickly and then spoke to his companion, a boy even younger than himself, just fifteen years old.

'Klaus, I'm going to take a look inside. You look around the site, maybe you'll find something interesting.'

Klaus was disappointed. 'Can't I go inside, too?'

'You will. After I'm done.'

Adolph walked around the fuselage. The glass of the bombardier's blister under the nose was broken but that of the forward gunner's with its two guns pointing toward the sky was intact.

Large and small chunks of metal were scattered all around as well as a huge wheel, fallen on its side.

The fuselage door was open. Adolph took out his service torchlight, switched it on and stepped inside.

It was like playing cowboys and Indians just as in one of his favourite Karl May stories, only this was real and infinitely more exciting.

He moved deeper into the interior, lighting his way with his torchlight until he reached the cockpit. It was leaning over to one side

---

[11]   The young members of the *Hitlerjügend* were usually the first to explore the wreckages of downed aircraft.

as was the whole aircraft. Most of the gauges and indicators on the flying panel were broken. Adolph sat in the pilot's seat and tried to shift the joystick but it was stuck. What was it like, flying such an airplane at night? What was it like to fly, free from the earth's bounds? Adolph, just a village boy, had never flown. The closest he had ever been to an airplane was the wreckage of the three aircraft that had been downed close to his village. He decided that when he turned 18 in two years he would enlist to become a pilot in the Luftwaffe.

Hearing Klaus' voice, he rose from the pilot's seat.

'Can I come in?'

'Yes, but watch your head. It's low.'

Adolph returned to the cockpit and sat at the navigation desk. He could see clearly in the light of day. He noted the gauges, the switches and the large, broken display that dominated. Something rustled under his foot. Adolph looked down and saw a chart. He picked it up. This was certainly very important.

Klaus joined him and sat down next to him. He also looked over the gauges, the switches and the large display.

'I wonder what that is?' he asked.

'I don't know, Klaus. I've never seen anything like it...'

Adolph remained a little longer going over everything again and again, trying to retain what he saw so that he could write up his report. Then he followed Klaus out of the plane. He walked around the aircraft one last time.

He noticed the big bulge under the fuselage. Looking closely, he saw that its metal cover had been sheared open in the crash leaving a large rent the size of a football. He knelt down and peered inside.

He saw a mass of wires, equipment, broken glass, a jumbled mess. He had no idea what he was looking at but he was sure that it was important. He would try to describe it as clearly as he could in his report.

They made another tour of the Lancaster and examined the debris scattered all over the field without finding anything more that attracted their interest.

'Let's go back, Klaus.'

Adolf was feeling the first pangs of hunger as in his eagerness to explore the crash site, he hadn't even paused for breakfast. He would have it now at home, while writing up his report.

The local leader of the *Hitlerjügend* would decide if his report was worth forwarding to higher circles.

• • •

'On the night of December 29, 712 bombers targeted the centre of Berlin. And were successful. Aerial photographs from the next day show that damage was extensive. We lost 11 aircraft. Among them...' The head of MI6, Sir Stewart Menzies[12] paused and glanced at the report on his

---

[12]　Stewart Menzies was head of MI6 (Military Intelligence 6, also known as the Secret Intelligence Service or SIS). Its mission was to gather intelligence from abroad. In his James Bond novels, Ian Fleming used the initial M from Menzies' surname even though he gave his character additional details drawn from an acquaintance of his, Admiral Sir Miles Messervy, head of Naval Intelligence. Menzies himself actually signed with a C, honouring the tradition established by the head of MI6 during WWI, Cummings. MI5 was the counter-espionage service. There was also an MI9, created to track down escaped prisoners of war.

desk. '...was a Lancaster of the Australian Squadron 460 out of the base at Binbrook, code name AR-N and number JB 607. It was equipped with the new model of the H2S, whatever this H2S stands for...'[13]

'"Home Sweet Home",' Andrew Bond said

'What's that, Bond?'

'The acronym H2S, sir. Airmen claim that it comes from the phrase Home Sweet Home because it helps them find their way back home in the night.'

'Thanks for enlightening me,' Menzies commented drily before continuing.

'It's the worst luck that one of the first bombers to carry the new H2S should be shot down so soon. I imagine it would have happened sooner or later. It was unavoidable. According to the experts, it will take the Germans at least six months studying the remains of the apparatus to come up with countermeasures. In six months, Harris is sure that without German interference, we can destroy whatever German cities remain, Leipzig, Dresden, Munich, Frankfurt on Oder, Erfurt, etc.'[14]

---

[13]　An actual event.

[14]　In May of 1943, a Halifax was shot down near Rotterdam, carrying an H2S MKI. The German expert at Telefunken, Otto Hachenberg, examined the *Rotterdam Gerät*, as the Germans named it, and even met with captured British airmen, some of whom were less than discrete, allowing some critical information to slip out. Hachenberg wrote a report with a detailed description of the H2S, describing each of its parts and functions except for the transmitter-receiver and the cathode tube which had carried a small explosive charge that destroyed it. Up to the end of the war, the Germans were never able to develop effective countermeasures against the H2S MKIII, nor the model that followed which operated at a wavelength of 1.5cms which was so effective that it could even show raincloud formations on the display.

'There is one problem, though: Squadron Leader Rodger. His real name is Paul Jenkins, Lecturer at the Physics Department at the University of Birmingham.' C referred to his notes. 'He's part of the team of J. T. Randall and A. H. Boot, colleagues of Professor M. L. E. Oliphant...I assume the name Oliphant is familiar to you...'

'His research team was assigned the contract from the Committee for the Coordination of Valve Development to develop a means of emitting radio waves at low frequencies. The research led to the invention of the cavity magnetron...'[15]

'Precisely, Bond. And the electronic war between us and the Germans is unending. It appears that Jenkins decided to try out himself the latest version of this H2S apparatus under real-life conditions while at the same time, instructing two Pathfinder radar operators in its use. He found himself in the lead Pathfinder of Squadron 460, which happened to be one of the first equipped with the new H2S. All this, of course, without the knowledge, let alone approval, of Harris[16] or of Oliphant. What a blunder! We've just been informed through the Red Cross that Jenkins sent a first card,[17] saying he survived the crash and is alive and well and a prisoner of war in *Stalag Luft III*[18]. This news has caused many of us to lose a lot of sleep. It might have been better if Jenkins hadn't survived. It's a real mess!'

---

[15] Actual persons and events.

[16] Sir Arthur Harris, Air Vice Marshal, head of RAF's Bomber Command, a proponent of night-time area bombing of population centres. Known as Bomber to his friends, Butcher to his adversaries.

[17] Prisoners of war had the right to send three cards a month to their families through the Red Cross.

[18] Prisoner of war camp for Air Force personnel.

C drew on his pipe, one of his few known vices that had survived the shortages of wartime. In any event, he had the excuse that he was only following the example of Churchill, who did not deprive himself of his cigars.

'You can understand the concern. If the Germans learn of Jenkins' true identity they'll try to make him talk and you know how effective the methods of the SS and Gestapo can be. No Geneva Convention will stand in their way. The Germans as a rule treat their POW's quite decently, and the Luftwaffe treats our boys, British and Americans, even better. But if he's discovered, out the window goes the Geneva Convention and any rights of prisoner of war status. They'll pull him out of the Luftwaffe's jurisdiction and no one can stop them.'

C tapped some ash out of his pipe.

'Yesterday I received two calls. One from Bomber Harris himself, in a rage, and the other from Professor Oliphant, close to hysteria. They both emphasised that this cannot be allowed to happen, and it's our job to prevent it. I don't know who they think we are, Bond. Do they think we have supernatural powers? But I do see their point. The fate of Bomber Command's future operations is at stake here.'

C stared directly at Bond as he continued.

'I can see just one solution. Delicate...difficult...Bond, this time I'm not ordering you...purely voluntary...due to the nature of this mission, I'll understand if you don't accept.'

Bond was silent.

'The only way is to send in one of ours to Jenkins. He would parachute down in the guise of an officer of a downed aircraft. Officers all end up in *Stalag Luft III*. His job would be to take

Jenkins under his wing, protect him and keep him out of the Gestapo's hands. And to attempt to escape with him and bring him back. But under no circumstances can he be allowed to fall into the hands of the SS and the Gestapo. You do understand what I'm saying, Bond?'

'Guardian…or exterminating angel, sir. I understand completely.'

C rose and gazed out of the window of his office on the fifth floor of the building on the corner of St. James and Broadway, a little beyond Victoria Station, near the St. James Park Underground. A grey day in late January, very usual for London. But relatively calm for a change. By now, visits by the Luftwaffe bombers had become very rare, a few at night, practically none during daylight in cloudy conditions – a Focke-Wulf 190 fighter-bomber perhaps, minor nuisances, like an annoying mosquito, nothing more. While at the same time, the cities of Germany were being turned into heaps of rubble by the RAF and, increasingly, by the American 8th Army Air Force by day.

With his back to Bond, he said, 'You can think about it before you decide. Until tonight.'

'No need, sir. Someone has to do it. I accept.'

C turned around, relieved, though he didn't show it. Someone definitely had to do it and the best man for the job, his first choice, was Andrew Bond.

'Very well, Bond,' he said. 'You have several advantages for this mission: your German is excellent, you know Germany well enough and, from your experience in sailing and flying, you have the rudiments of navigation so you can pass as your cover - an RAF navigator. We'll get you the latest information on *Stalag Luft III*, update you on the situation today in Germany. You have one week to prepare before the next RAF mission. You can log in a few hours of training in the basics of navigation with the RAF. I'll arrange a meeting for you with Oliver Philpot.[19] He managed to escape from the camp in November and make his way back through Sweden. He can brief you on what he encountered. And J will put together a package of a few items that might come in useful. Anything else?'

'No, sir.'

'Okay, Bond. Before you leave, you'll brief me on your plan. For a possible escape, I mean.'

'Of course, sir.'

Bond rose and left C's office. C lingered a little while longer looking out the window…he was sending his best agent to imprisonment, possibly death…and possibly the death of another as well…and he had burdened him with an ethical dilemma that he himself hoped he would never have to face. What nonsense, what hypocrisy, he thought. He himself was the ethical instigator. But perhaps things wouldn't turn out that badly. Perhaps the Germans will never suspect anything and Bond would spend the rest of the war as a prisoner. It wouldn't be for much longer anyway. Or, maybe he does manage to escape, like Philpot had. If anyone had the capability, it was Bond. And he had one more important advantage, crucial in wartime: luck. He was going to need it.

---

[19]　Actual person and a true story, the escape of three officers, the famous Wooden Horse incident. See Carrol.

C returned to his desk and sat down. Drawing deeply on his pipe, he opened the next file on his desk.

• • •

In the Savoy Bar, Bond drained the remnants of his Martini, as usual, shaken, not stirred, while Philpot finished his second whiskey.

Philpot had described in detail the story of his escape, answering each of Bond's questions. He hadn't asked what Bond's interest was, nor even his name, since the request for the meeting had come down to him through channels as an order. He assumed the man he was talking to was from MI9, just like the others he had met with in London after his escape.

'Keep in mind, though,' continued Philpot. 'If someone were to escape today, I wouldn't advise following our route, travelling by train toward the Baltic ports and then by ferry to Sweden. We were the lucky first. German patrolling of the ports must be far more thorough now.'

• • •

J set down a pair of boots on his worktable.

'Boots, RAF standard issue,' he declared. 'Though, with a few useful adjustments…'

He picked up the right boot and slid aside the heel revealing a small cavity. He removed a lighter from the cavity, showed it to Bond, and replaced it. He then slid open the sole.

'Now turn the boot around, Bond.'

Inside Bond found a very thin razor-sharp blade about 10cm long with a tiny bolt next to it.

J slid the sole back in place and picked up the left boot. Again, he slid open the sole, revealing a very thin knife shaft with a hole at one end.

'Bolt the two pieces together and that gives you a very effective little weapon,' he explained unnecessarily.

He then slid open the heel of the left boot and showed its contents to Bond.

'Your treasury. Ten gold sovereigns. Very much in demand in the Third Reich, I'm told.'

Bond noted the sovereigns nestled tightly in twos in the five cutouts.

J closed the boots' soles and heels and handed one to Bond.

'Feel inside. It's specially lined to protect from the cold. Very practical.'

Then, almost without a sound, he pulled out the innersole of one of the boots and showed Bond what was inside.

'In here you have your papers, travel documents, identification, even food ration coupons, all of it authentic, except for your photograph of course, which we added. For your friend…we have additional documents, all you have to do is to add dates where required. I'll show you where and how later…All this, courtesy of POW's from the Italian Front and our informants in the Reich. Most of the documents are valid for a time once the date is inserted. Observe how the innersole fits back into place.'

J picked up the other boot and repeated the process, extracted its innersole, retrieving what appeared to be a folded silk handkerchief. He opened it up on the worktable to reveal a large map of Germany.

'Parachute silk,' he said. 'Finer than paper, more durable. It doesn't rustle nor does it tear easily.'

He dug his hand even deeper into the shoe, searching with his fingers and took out a small packet wrapped in silk. He opened it to reveal a tiny compass no larger than a watch face.

'We fashioned it out of a wristwatch. The points and hand are phosphorescent so they will be visible at night. Ah! Lest I forget! Here, Bond…' He showed him the inside of the boot.

Bond made out what looked like banknotes.

'Authentic *Reichsmarks*, offered by our Wehrmacht prisoners. That's it, Bond. I hope everything will prove useful.'

'J,' Bond laughed. 'You are a true genius.'

'I know,' J replied with some condescension.

As Bond left, J called out, 'Bond, don't you go losing those boots, now!'

• • •

'Ready, sir!' the Lancaster's upper gunner shouted out to Bond. He opened the rear door of the aircraft.

Bond took two steps forward, reaching the door. He felt the cold wind in his face as he grabbed hold of both sides of the opening.

'Go!' shouted the gunner over the roar of the engines.

Bond pushed with his hands and jumped into the void. He felt the familiar rush of free fall, as if he were floating in a celestial sea, absolute calm, weightless, free of earthly constraints. He reached for the ripcord and pulled it. He felt the sharp tug as the canopy unfolded above him and he began to float downward toward the dark earth.

At the moment of impact, he bent his knees and rolled to reduce the shock as he had learnt to do during SAS training.[20]

He got up, shook off his parachute's harness and scanned the area.

He found himself in a field at whose edge he could make out some scattered trees. Around him, in the darkness, more of the same: fields, trees here and there. No dwellings, not even any farm buildings and, of course, no lights anywhere because of the blackout. No roads, no paths nor any power poles. Where had he landed?

He looked at his watch. At least four hours until dawn. No need to hurry. He made his way to the nearest cluster of trees and sat under one, leaning against the trunk. It was horrendously cold, but there was no snow. The cold, that devious enemy, penetrated even further into his body, despite the warm RAF kit. It had also been icy cold in the bomber because of the height at which those aircraft flew. Their heating systems were never effective at keeping the cold at bay.

An hour passed. He rose, took a few steps, shook his arms for a few moments to warm up a little and then looked around for better shelter. He found a spot where some wild ferns were growing that had kept the ground underneath dry. He sat down on the ferns with his back against a tree and, uprooting some, covered himself with them to act as a blanket. He closed his eyes…

---

[20]   Special Air Service. Created in 1942 as a Special Forces unit in North Africa. SAS units have taken part in all of Great Britain's wars since then.

He woke with a start, realizing he had fallen asleep. First light had awakened him. Despite the ferns, he was freezing. He got up, left the cover of the trees and scanned the terrain again. In the morning light he could see he was in a flat valley, fields all around. He could make out some hills in the distance with thicker vegetation and some patches of snow. He spotted a dirt road about 100 yards away and, in the distance, about a mile further on, a building that looked like a barn.

A dirt road. It must lead somewhere, he thought. Bond smiled to himself. He would never have imagined that it would be so difficult to allow himself to be captured and taken prisoner.

He began to walk as the daylight increased. It was a cloudy, gloomy day, but at least it wasn't raining. His clothes, however, were damp from the night frost. The brisk walk helped warm him.

The road wound its way up a small hill and as he reached the crest he could make out the houses of a village in the distance, about two kilometers away.

At last!

He made his way toward them.

The first person he encountered was a villager of around sixty walking toward him leading a tired-looking workhorse, probably on his way to his fields.

As they approached each other, Bond spoke: *'Guten Morgen!'*

'Guten Morgen!' came the reply from the farmer who simply continued on his way without a second glance.

Bond reached the edge of the village. The road passed through it. Two-storey houses, roofs steeply inclined for the snow, windows with pretty white embroidered curtains, some with flower arrangements inside, a few shops. There were no ruins. The war had not reached this place.

The village was awakening and people, children and the elderly were emerging from their homes.

Bond stopped and stood still. Wasn't anyone going to confront him? Wasn't he going to be arrested? Did he have to search out the nearest police station himself and turn himself in? Was there even a police station in this forgotten village?

He slowly walked toward the centre, the village square, with some people staring at him curiously, others nodding in greeting, but no one attempting to stop him.

His first encounter with the terrible might of the armed forces of the Third Reich was at the square and was in the form of a sixty-year-old of the *Landwehr*[21], limping slightly from a World War I wound. He brandished a WWI-era rifle. Under his ill-fitting uniform his belly was visible, unaffected by the restrictions of food rationing. He was accompanied by a lean young boy, a member of the *Hitlerjugend*, so thin that he looked almost malnourished.

Bond put his hands up.

He was led to the only *Bierstube*[22] on the square. Obviously there was no police station in this village. He sat at a table with the boy who observed him with uneasy curiosity while the *Landwehr* man made a telephone call.

The tavern keeper brought over a bottle of schnapps and two glasses, a plate with plenty of dark brown bread and another of

---

[21]   *Landwehr*: "Defence of the country", the Home Guard.
[22]   *Bierstube*: Beer tavern.

sausages. This village was obviously not wanting for any of the basic foods.

The *Landwehr* man finished his call and joined them. He sat down. He poured a glass of schnapps for Bond. The tavern keeper brought the boy a wooden cup of milk which he drank greedily. His captor offered him bread and sausages. Bond helped himself and started to eat. He was hungry, he hadn't eaten since before the takeoff from England the previous night.

Bond searched his pockets for the bar of chocolate all airmen carried with them, unwrapped it, put it on the table and pushed it toward the boy.

The boy stared at the treasure greedily. Real chocolate was a great luxury in Germany because of the Allied naval blockade. He hadn't had any chocolate since the beginning of the war. Nevertheless, he hesitated to accept the gift until the man said, 'Go ahead, Hans.'

The boy finally reached out, broke off a piece, stuffed it into his mouth and ate it, almost swallowing it whole like a hungry dog afraid it would be taken away.

Bond offered some to the man who broke off a small piece. He then offered the rest of the bar to the boy, leading him to understand that it was his to keep. This time there was no hesitation. The boy took, or, rather, grabbed it and shoved it into a pocket of his uniform.

They sat there for a while, the schnapps warming him up, enjoying the warmth of the tavern, exchanging just a few words, the Germans in their language, Bond in English. He wasn't willing to reveal that he spoke German. Eventually, around two hours later two *Wehrmacht* soldiers walked in, obviously sent by the authorities the *Landwehr* man had called earlier.

'*Komm!*'[23] they said.

Bond rose, exchanged goodbyes with the man, the boy and the tavern keeper and followed the two soldiers outside. They got into a *Kübelwagen*,[24] one soldier driving in front, the other with his rifle, seated in the back next to Bond.

They left the village, soon getting onto an asphalt road, passed several villages and towns and eventually reached the outskirts of a city. Bond assumed that it was Magdeburg since it was the largest city near his drop point.

This was confirmed when they drove up to the railway station. Escorted by one of the soldiers, he was boarded onto a train with the rest of the passengers, heading for Frankfurt. Even now, in the sixth year of the war, the Germans stuck to their bureaucratic procedures. Crew members of downed Allied aircraft were first sent to the *Dulag*[25] in Frankfurt to be interrogated, usually half-heartedly and with rare success, by Luftwaffe officers in the hope that they might learn something more than just name, rank and serial number, which was all POW's were obliged to divulge under the Geneva Convention. They were then funnelled to the various POW camps.

And so it went with Bond. His military escort handed him over to the Luftwaffe. Two officers interrogated him, offered him a cigarette, English coincidentally, spoils of war. Bond gave his rank

---

[23]   Come!

[24]   *Kübelwagen*: The German version of the Jeep.

[25]   *Dulag*: *Durchgangslager*, or transit camp.

as Flying Officer, the name Douglas Laidlaw, his serial number and nothing else.

He remained at the *Dulag* for a few hours until he and a group of other RAF officers were escorted back to the railway station, loaded on to a freight car and locked in.

The train began its torturous journey to the prison camp. At least now he had company and the hours passed somewhat faster until the doors were swung open when they reached their destination at last: the Sagan Railway Station, the closest to *Stalag Luft III*.

CHAPTER III

Tunnelling

The camp was situated in the middle of a forest. It was surrounded by two 9ft-high barbed wire fences, five feet apart. The area between them contained more fences that were not as high but were so dense one could barely see through them. Thirty feet into the camp was an "alarm wire", the point beyond which prisoners were not allowed. Every 150 feet was a wooden guard tower with a roof, equipped with floodlights. At night, guards with trained dogs patrolled the fence.

Inside the North Compound were 15 wooden barracks in three rows and a large flat area for the prisoners to mingle or report to for *Appel*, as the Germans called the rollcall.

Further north were the three buildings known as the *Vorlager*, the hospital, a warehouse and the "cooler", an isolation cell for punishing prisoners who attempted to escape or had committed some other offence.

To the south was the similar South Compound recently added to contain the ever-increasing numbers of American airmen.

Forest surrounded the camp. Austere, slender, tall fir trees, densely packed, like lances rising into the dull sky, immobile guardians, like a second zone of fencing rising from the grey earth. In every direction they could be seen, blocking off the horizon, a monotonous barrier that bred a feeling of isolation, of being cut off. Between the outer fence and the forest the Germans had created a no-man's-land, a barren stretch thirty feet wide denying cover for anyone attempting to escape through the fences.

Each barracks consisted of 18 rooms of $12m^2$ each for eight men and three smaller rooms for two men, intended for higher-ranking officers. Furniture was restricted to the basics: four two-level bunk beds, mattresses stuffed with straw and shredded newspapers, blankets, a table and eight chairs in the middle of each room, since the men also ate there. Each barracks also had a room with a cement floor with some sinks and shower stalls, a few toilets and a coal-fired kitchen stove with two burners and a small oven.

The Germans, all Luftwaffe personnel, processed the newcomers through the administration building, noting their names, ranks and serial numbers in their ledgers and then assigning them to their barracks.[26]

Prisoners would flock to greet the newcomers, some recognising comrades, eager for news from home and how the war was progressing. Several approached Bond, asking him about his unit and how he had been captured.

---

[26] The description of the camp, the life of the POW's, the description of "Harry", relations with the Germans are all real and are based on the books by Brickhill and Carrol. The German officer who lent the Leica to the prisoners was *Kapitän* Pieber.

Bond was aware, thanks to Philpot, that newcomers were held in suspicion until their identities were cross-checked and confirmed. Rumours abounded, never confirmed, that their captors frequently tried to pass off their own men as POW's to spy on the prisoners. Anyone who was not recognised by an older prisoner was quarantined and subjected to lengthy questioning by other officers until they were convinced he was not a plant.

Bond had no time to waste on such procedures. He found out where Squadron Leader Roger Bushell[27] was billeted and sought him out.

'Sir, I must talk to you privately.'

Bushell indicated with a nod for Bond to follow him to his room, one of the small, two-man rooms reserved for high-ranking officers. He had been a guest of the Luftwaffe for nearly four years so far, from the time his Spitfire had been shot down over Dunkirk in May 1940.

He also went by a second name: Big X. In essence and unofficially he was the Intelligence Officer of the camp, a kindred spirit of sorts.

'Greetings form Oliver Philpot,' Bond said once they were alone. 'And from Group Captain John Wilkins, the commander of the Lancaster that ferried me over.'

'Ah, John. We flew together in Squadron 601,' Bushell mused.

'Actually, you were both in the same year at Cranwell,'[28] Bond quickly corrected him, neatly evading the trap.

Bushell's eyebrows rose. He looked closely at Bond standing before him. He saw a man of around 25, grey-blue eyes with a trace of

---

27   Actual person.
28   The RAF (Cadet) College in Cranwell, now the Royal Air Force College.

hardness yet indicating a willingness to laugh and enjoy the pleasures of life, handsome, manly features, black hair, slightly over 6 feet tall. Definitely a ladies' man.

'Sit down,' he said, indicating the other chair at the table.

Bond sat. 'My name is Bond. Andrew Bond, Lieutenant Commander RNVR. Sir, what I have to say from this moment on in is in the strictest confidence. No one else must ever find out.'

Bushell was puzzled but didn't show it.

'I'm MI6,' Bond continued. 'I parachuted from a Lancaster under the false identity of an RAF officer to reach here. The purpose? To protect one of the prisoners in this camp, Squadron Leader Robert Rodger. His real name is Jenkins, Paul Jenkins. He's a Lecturer at the University of Birmingham.'

Bond described briefly how Jenkins had found himself at *Stalag Luft III* and the reason his real identity had to remain secret. When he finished, Bushell remained silent. The story he had just heard seemed fantastic, crazy. So crazy in fact that it seemed very unlikely that anyone could possibly have dreamed it up, especially the Germans, who were not known for their imagination. Also, what he had just been told did, in fact, serve to resolve some his earlier doubts.

'I've met with Rodger,' he said. 'We quarantined him because he seemed a little odd. Suspicious. He couldn't even remember his aircraft's tail number! On the other hand, he was very much up on his electronics, as some of our navigators confirmed. But, beyond that, why should I believe you?'

'Why would I invent such a story? For what reason?'

'Indeed. Why?'

'Allow me, sir,' Bond said.

He leaned down and removed his right boot, placing it on the table in front of the astonished Bushell. He took out the innersole, removed his documents and laid them out in front of Bushell.

'I know that you also prepare false documents here for escape attempts. Philpot told me. But these papers are authentic, from German POW's and other sources, with my photograph inserted. As you well know, sir, these aren't standard RAF issue for its crewmembers.'

Speechless, Bushell examined the documents. With his experience and having seen authentic German documents belonging to the camp guards, he was convinced that these were genuine.

'So what do you want from me, Bond?'

'First, your personal stamp of approval so that I won't lose any time with the quarantine process. Second, your assurance that, after I find Jenkins, you'll meet with both of us together.'

Bond looked Bushell straight in the eye and continued.

'Third, absolute priority in any escape attempts. Philpot informed me there are such plans…'

'Okay, Bond. Find Jenkins. Then we'll see.'

Bond spent an hour searching among the prisoners, most of whom were outside the barracks. A few were tending to vegetable patches, others were sitting on the ground reading, while others were rehearsing a play on a hastily-put-together set they had built with supplies provided by the guards. Others were playing football, cheered on by their mates, some were exercising, while others simply stood around or walked about in groups, chatting.

Bond knew what Jenkins looked like from photographs but also realised that even in this restricted space, finding him among more than a thousand men would not be easy. He finally found him walking with three airmen and approached him:

'Squadron Leader Rodger?'

The men stared at him. This newcomer was unfamiliar. 'Yes?'

'Can I have a word with you?'

Jenkins was puzzled but didn't refuse. Any chance to talk to someone new was a break in the monotony. Jenkins had only been a prisoner for a month and a half but the boredom and inactivity made it seem that many months had gone by.

They stepped away from the others, and walked in silence to the edge of the camp, near the "alert wire", a good distance from the nearest prisoners so that they would not be overheard. From one of the towers, fifty feet away, a German guard was looking in their direction but couldn't possibly hear what they were saying from that distance, even if he did happen to understand English.

'Professor Jenkins, my name is Bond.'

Astonishment showed on the man's face at hearing his real name spoken. Bond didn't give him a chance to respond, quickly launching into an explanation of who he was and why he was there.

Just as Bushell had been earlier, Jenkins was suspicious and wary at first. But after Bond answered all his questions properly, including details that no one else could have known, the professor was convinced. Bond had prepared himself well, thanks to the material that MI6 had gathered for him.

'Who else is aware of my true identity?' Jenkins asked.

'Only Bushell. And it was necessary. No one else, and it will stay that way. Now let's go talk to him.'

They met with Bushell in the latter's room and Jenkins confirmed his real identity. Bushell arranged that they bunk together with the excuse that they were old acquaintances, with Bond on the bottom bunk and Jenkins on the top one.

Once again, Bond posed the question that was constantly on his mind. 'How are current escape plans coming along?'

For the first time, Bushell smiled.

'You're an impatient man, Bond. You must learn the virtues of patience and endurance. Anyway. How are you at digging?'

And that's how Bond met Harry.

• • •

Sturmbannführer[29] Benno Fiala Ritter von Fernbrugg was not a technology expert. He belonged to Subdirectorate B, Espionage, West, of the External Affairs Section of the Security Department of the Reich's Ministry of Defence.

So when his superior, Walter Schellenberg,[30] the section head, assigned him his new duties at the suggestion of Himmler himself, he was puzzled and somewhat intimidated by the challenge.

'Himmler himself believes in you,' Schellenberg said to him. 'So do I. You'll manage. You don't need any technical background, you

---

[29]   SS rank equivalent to major.
[30]   Historical figure.

just need an analytical mind and police knowhow, and you certainly do have those.'

Benno was puzzled for another reason as well: this kind of job was actually the responsibility of the technical personnel of the *Luftwaffe* and the *Abwehr* of Admiral Canaris.[31] But after some thought, he understood. By now, Benno was familiar with the labyrinthine corridors of power within the Third Reich, the rivalries and the hatreds of the protagonists, the plots and counterplots, the intrigues to win the trust and a position next to Hitler. Recently, the second place in the hierarchy which once belonged to Goering was undecided. Hitler had tired of his bloated promises about the *Luftwaffe*, that it would win the Battle of Britain, that London and other British cities would be levelled (the *Führer* had believed him then and had declaimed that 'they would erase those cities from the map' only to be betrayed and ridiculed), and that it would protect the cities of Germany from Allied bombs. As for Canaris, an aristocrat and admiral, Hitler never particularly trusted him or, for that manner, any of his other admirals of the old school.

That left Himmler, who was gaining ground with his SS. And Himmler knew just how to take advantage of every opportunity and to create new ones, each time pounding yet another nail into the coffin of Goering's standing which was being eroded anyway with every bomb that fell on a German city, especially on Berlin.

---

[31]   *Abwehr*: The German counter-espionage service. The ambivalent Admiral Canaris was its head until the July 1944 plot against Hitler. He was suspected to having played a part in it and was executed.

Hence the mission entrusted to Benno. He was quickly briefed, studying the files all through the night, fuelled with cigarettes and cognac supplied by his aide, *Oberscarführer*[32] Oskar Frühauf.

He began to put together a plan of action. He realized his superior had been right. He didn't need any technical knowledge, just German thoroughness and diligence would suffice. Or, rather, Austrian. In spite of the fact that Austria was now part of the Third Reich, Benno never forgot that he was Austrian, as was, for that matter, the *Führer* himself. His family had over the centuries given the Austro-Hungarian Army many officers, such as an uncle with the same name, an ace of the Austro-Hungarian Air Force with 28 victories.[33]

• • •

Bond wrote the first card he was allowed to send out, to be delivered by the Red Cross, destination: C.

"Dear Aunt Clara,

I am well, don't worry about me. The Germans are treating us very well. I read, exercise and grow vegetables. Take care of Uncle Paul's health."

The "grow vegetables" reference indicated that there was an escape plan in progress. The reference to Uncle Paul was a confirmation that contact had been made with the professor.

After that, Bond went to Harry.

---

[32]   SS rank equivalent to sergeant.

[33]   Historical figure.

The tunnel that had been named Harry was one of three that the prisoners had begun to dig and it was an ingenious marvel of inspiration and improvisation. First of all, its access, artfully hidden under the coal stove in Barracks 104 was invisible to the camp guards, who were prone to making frequent spot checks.

The stove was pushed back, revealing the ladder that seemed to lead down into the bowels of the earth. Bond descended after one of the older prisoners.

At the bottom was another technical feat, a chamber dug out of the clay earth that was large enough for men to stand in and work upright. It served as a storage area for their tools, many handcrafted, others stolen from the Germans. It also housed the makeshift pump that provided air for the diggers excavating the tunnel. The air duct was buried under the tunnel floor. It was made of milk tins with their tops and bottoms removed, joined together. From the storage chamber, the tunnel began its horizontal journey that would lead outside the camp.

A second ingenious inspiration: a rail track on the tunnel floor, constructed of wood. A small flat trolley ran along it allowing a man to travel on it only lying face down as the tunnel's ceiling was very low in order to save on time and materials. Throughout the length of the tunnel, the ceiling was supported by wooden slats from the bunk beds because, though the sandy, clay earth was easy to dig through, it was prone to collapsing.

'Welcome to Harry!' one of the men below said, handing him a tool, something between a homemade hoe and shovel, as he gave him his instructions. The men showed him how to stretch out on the trolley.

'Ready?'

'Ready!'

The men began pulling on the rope that was attached by pulley to the trolley. Bond entered the tunnel. He expected darkness, but here again was yet another surprise: it was lit up by light bulbs strung along a cable obviously stolen from the Germans. He learned later that the prisoners had managed to connect it to the camp's electrical supply.

At one point in the tunnel, the prisoners had dug out a chamber they had named "Piccadilly Circus" and further down, estimated to be under the "cooler", was a second one, called "Leicester Square". After a short distance, he came face to face with the tunnel's end, a wall of unstable packed earth. On his belly, he began digging cautiously with the makeshift tool he had been given. When he had gathered a sufficient amount of earth, he filled up a sack and passed it back to his helper, lying on a second trolley behind him.

It was exhausting work in the cramped space, lying there uncomfortably, the atmosphere stifling, despite the ventilation. Very soon he was drenched in sweat, naked as he was, as were all the diggers, so as to be unencumbered by clothing and also to avoid getting their clothes dirty and betraying their activities to the Germans.

He was relieved when, after an hour, he felt a tug on the trolley indicating his shift was over and he was to be dragged back for the next man to take over.

Pulled back to first chamber, he climbed up the ladder leaving behind the claustrophobic atmosphere, showered, wiped himself dry and put on his clothes.

In the days that followed, while the digging went on and the tunnel lengthened, Bond familiarised himself with all the camp's secrets. He explained the basics of the escape plan to Jenkins. They decided to practice speaking in French to each other to be able to pass as French (as long as they didn't encounter an actual Frenchman). Jenkins spoke it well enough, Bond more fluently.

Bond learned about the various special "services" provided by the prisoners: for example, there was Bushell's own counterespionage-espionage X service that kept watch on the guards to warn of any impending spot raids. This service also gathered information crucial for the escape: by now they were familiar with all the trails that led through the forest to Sagan, the lay of the land in general, even the schedules of the trains leaving Sagan. Bond compared this information with what he had been given before leaving England. It coincided. All this information had been garnered principally from certain camp guards, the "domesticated ferrets". The prisoners referred to the guards as "ferrets" and those with whom they had developed some special connection, either of a friendly or commercial nature, were deemed "domesticated". Bribery between prisoners and guards was rampant. The prisoners had many assets coveted by their guards. The parcels they received through the Red Cross contained cigarettes, tins of milk and corned beef, chocolate, coffee and sugar, all rarities in Germany. By some measure, the prisoners were better off than the guards. The spare diet consisted of potatoes, vegetable soup with very little meat or fat, black bread. This diet afforded them 1,500-1,900 calories when an average man required 3,000. And the guards' diet was no better. The contents of the Red Cross parcels helped, but in fact all the men had lost weight since entering the camp. One could frequently tell how long a prisoner had been in the camp by his weight and the appearance and colour of his skin. The older ones had acquired a dry, yellowish skin resembling fragile ancient parchment. With the domesticated German guards, the prisoners exchanged cigarettes, chocolate, coffee and sugar for information and the various supplies they required.

There was a tailoring service, altering uniforms into civilian clothing: the domesticated ferrets would receive cigarettes in exchange for buttons: 'Hey, Werner! I lost one of the buttons off my uniform…can you find me one? Better yet, three, so that I won't have to bother you again if I lose another one…and some thread…here's a pack of cigarettes.'

It was odd how frequently buttons were being lost in the sandy ground of the camp, as if the men who were cultivating vegetables (and carefully spreading the dirt excavated from Harry brought to them hidden in bags under the men's trousers) were planting buttons instead of seeds!

There was also a forgery service, charged with preparing false documents for the prisoners - with current photographs, courtesy of a German officer who had lent them a Leica camera, ostensibly for artistic purposes. It was this service that would enter the correct dates on Bond's documents to validate them.

The technical service manufactured anything from compasses to wire cutters, the latter no longer necessary now that the current escape plan was to tunnel under the fences.

From one of the "domesticated" Germans, Bond was able to obtain two pairs of civilian shoes, for himself and for Jenkins: 'Wolfgang, my boots are just too heavy for daily wear now that spring is upon us. They've damaged my feet. Can you find me two pairs of shoes, for me and my friend? Size? 43-44 and 42-43. You chose the colour…yes… cigarettes, sugar, coffee…and, okay, three tins of milk…and tea? Didn't know you liked it. You're adopting English habits, Wolfgang! Right, five boxes of tea as well - and Indian tea, at that!'

Civilian shoes were absolutely necessary and it was impossible to convert boots convincingly into shoes.

The days passed, digging, planning, with impatience and anticipation. Every day invisible Harry grew longer by a few feet and was now estimated to be under the fence. A few days more, a few dozen feet and the path to freedom would be open.

Bushell and the prisoner leadership, were in a hurry. They were concerned that the Germans would discover the camouflaged entrance to the tunnel under the stove as had been the case with prior efforts and that the escape would be squashed before it even began, now, when they were so close. It was estimated that they would be ready by mid-March, even though the weather would not be ideal, especially for those attempting to travel on foot. The cold, snow and rain would make their efforts especially difficult. But if they were to postpone for another month, the risk of discovery would just be too great.

Bond was in complete agreement. The inactivity, aside from the digging, and the boredom of camp life was getting to him. He was not used to being confined, and the living conditions in the camp, always the same view, the same measured steps from one point to another, made him feel like a caged animal. So he kept digging with vigour along with the others, spoke frequently with Jenkins and went over the details of the escape plan in his head again and again, even though he realised that many of the decisions would have to be made on the spur of the moment, depending on circumstances and sheer luck.

● ● ●

Benno pushed aside the reports, raised his head and stared at the wall opposite his desk which was covered with a large map of the Third Reich, just as he had ordered.

He had reached his initial conclusions. He felt that everything began with the bombing raid on the night of December 29. On that night, for the first time, the British bombers had hit the centre of Berlin with extraordinary accuracy, causing extensive damage and yet another outburst of rage by Hitler. It was that rampage, Benno surmised, that had given Himmler the opportunity to intervene and get his services involved.

How had the British managed that?

Benno had come to the conclusion that they had used a new navigation system, much more precise than the previous ones. Perhaps an improved version of the Rotterdam. In addition to the issue of accuracy, his hypothesis was also based on another fact, insignificant on its own, but crucial in conjunction with the fuller picture.

He recalled the report from a *Luftwaffe* crew on that night: they had spotted and downed a Lancaster. The radar operator of the fighter had tried to locate the Lancaster with his Naxos system which had always responded to signals from the Rotterdam, but without success. And yet, during the final attack, he had clearly seen the radome attached to the underbelly of the Lancaster. This had been confirmed by the pilot, Schnaufer. Had the operator not used the Naxos correctly? Unlikely, as he was one of the most experienced radar operators and had used it successfully many times.

Was the bomber's radar not active at the time of the attack? A possibility, perhaps, but not a likely one. The British used their radar to find their way home from the Reich until they were within reach of the range of their land-based systems. And, according to the reports he had received, the attack occurred before the Lancaster had reached that point. As a result, he had come to the conclusion that the English were using a new type of Rotterdam device which emitted at other frequencies.

Which ones, though?

That was the big question. And its answer would be crucial to whether or not the Reich's technical experts would be able to develop countermeasures quickly enough.

On the map opposite him, coloured pins marked the crash sites of the eleven enemy bombers that had been shot down that night. Three of them, those marked with red pins, after searching the wreckages, were determined to have been outfitted with the Rotterdam. The others, marked with yellow pins, had not been. And, according to another report, one of the three Lancasters was in fact shot down by a fighter using its Naxos. That British bomber had obviously been using the old model Rotterdam. Of the other two, the one was shot down by Schnaufer and the other had been downed by flak[34] since there had been no fighter reported in the vicinity of its downing.

Luftwaffe experts had examined the wrecks after reports from the first witnesses on site, *Hitlerjugend* members. They were convinced that all three aircraft had been equipped with the Rotterdam apparatus. But the radomes had been so badly damaged in the crashes that it was impossible to detect any differences between them, if there had been any. From the mass of crushed, half-burned parts, cables and broken glass there was no way of determining the frequency at which the devices operated.

Benno sighed.

As a policeman, regardless of the fact that he was a member of the SS, he knew something was missing: the human factor, human intelligence. If he could interrogate a British operator of the new Rotterdam, he might be able to find out what he was looking for. A very small yet huge step, just a number.

The operating frequency of the new Rotterdam.

But he didn't have one.

Could he find one?

How?

He sat there staring at the map, obsessed by that one question: how?

It was as if the mute map was mocking him. Eight yellow, three red pins…three red… three red!

---

34   *Flugabwehrkanone:* Anti-aircraft guns

'Dammit!' He banged his fist on the desk, shaking the overflowing ashtray and the full glass of cognac that he hadn't even touched. A little cognac spilled onto the desk, mingling with some of the ashes and creating a small pool of thick, reddish-grey liquid.

'Oskar!' he called out for his aide. 'Oskar!'

He was so excited by his sudden inspiration that he forgot to use the intercom.

Oskar opened the door.

'*Herr Sturmbannführer?*'

'Oskar, I have an idea. We need human intelligence. How are we going to get it?'

He pointed at the map, rose from his desk excitedly, approached it and touched two of the red pins.

'These two bombers are the key. We have to find out if there are any surviving officers. The Rotterdam operators are always officers, Oskar!'

Oskar remained silent.

'And if there were any survivors, I'm sure we'll find a Rotterdam operator among them. And why do I believe that, Oskar?'

Benno, in his excitement, wanted to impress his aide.

'Why, sir?'

'Because each Lancaster carries a seven-man crew. The two gunners and the wireless operators are always non-commissioned officers. So, that leaves four officers. Correct?'

'Correct, sir,' Oskar replied, though he still didn't get it.

'I've found in one of these Luftwaffe reports another seemingly insignificant fact which, as it turns out, is crucial. It's difficult to bail out of a disabled Lancaster. The survival rate is lower than with other craft.[35] So when a Lancaster is hit, the bailout sequence begins with the Rotterdam operator. As a result, the survival rate for the operator is higher since he bails out first. Simple statistics, Oskar, you see?' Benno felt very proud of himself.

'*Jawohl, mein Herr!*' Oskar said, though obviously still not grasping what all this had to do with the case.

'In other words, if there are any surviving officers from those two Lancasters, there's a big chance that one of them is our man. That's who we have to track down. You see, Oskar?'

'Yes, sir! I do!' Oskar agreed with his boss. He had already given up trying to understand. He had long ago decided simply to put his trust in his superior's logic.

'It's a pity that the Geneva Convention doesn't require officers to state their specialty. That would make it easier for us. Anyway, let's first track down the survivors, if any. Send out a message to the heads of the SS and the *Jugend* of the *Gau*[36] where the crashes occurred. Have them inform us if any officers were captured that night. Then, with that information, contact the *Luftwaffe* to get the names of those officers and to which camp they were transferred. Then we'll take over from there!'

Oskar prepared to leave, but was stopped by Benno.

'And one thing more, so we don't waste any time: locate all the camps for *Luftwaffe*'s POW's who are officers. We'll send one of our men to each commandant with the excuse of carrying out a security

---

[35]   A fact. This was one of the few weaknesses of the Lancaster.

[36]   Germany under the Nazi regime was divided into districts known as *Gau* headed by *Gauleiters*.

check. Our men will really be there to gather any information on whether any navigators are imprisoned there. I'm sure there are many, but we're only interested in those brought in on that one specific night. We must stress the importance of our mission to the commandant: any camp guard who has established some degree of trust with any of the prisoners must try to obtain this information.

'That's not something that will please *Herr* Göring,' Oskar smiled at the idea, not unfamiliar with the power struggles within the Reich.

'Not at all! But let him try and stop us. It will be give an additional edge to us and our leader. Whom should we send?'

Oskar thought for a while before replying, '*Sturmbannführers* Brunner[37] and Voigt. I think they would be the most suited. But I'll look into our personnel files to see who else we can send.'

'Yes, those are good choices. Find others also. You have until tomorrow! That's all for now.'

Oskar clicked his heels and cried out '*Heil* Hitler!', as he always did, even when he was alone with his superior. He always abided by the regulations of the Party and its hierarchy.

• • •

The arrival of the Horch[38] and the sight of the man in an SS uniform that stepped out of it caused a commotion in the camp. The

---

[37]   Historical figure. His visit to *Stalag Luft III* occurred in February 1944.

[38]   Horch: "listen": a luxury automobile brand, the precursor of Audi ("listen" in Latin). Since the Horch plant ended up in East Germany after the war, it was re-established as Audi in the West.

camp guards all stood at attention, saluting as the SS officer entered the Administration Building, where he remained for some time.

Bushell put all the prisoners who had developed special relations with domesticated ferrets to find out what was up.

'Who's the commandant's visitor, Wolfgang? Why such a stir?' Bond asked casually, offering the guard a cigarette.

'An SS major. Sent to examine camp security.' He took a deep drag off his cigarette, a real blend, not the ersatz version supplied to German soldiers, and continued conspiratorially:

'The commandant was not at all pleased. This camp is under the jurisdiction of the *Luftwaffe*. We're all *Luftwaffe*,' he added with some pride. 'What are these SS parasites up to getting underfoot? The commandant doesn't like them at all. None of us like them! But what can he do? The major has clearance signed by Göring himself.'

Wolfgang enjoyed another drag of his cigarette again before continuing.

'Of course, he found nothing. Can you imagine that!' he continued in acceptable English, which had improved considerably after conversing with British airman over the past two years as a camp guard.

'This camp was constructed so no one could escape, not even a fly. Isn't that so, Herr Peter?' He added, using Bond's cover name as a supposed RAF officer.

'Unfortunately, I must agree with you, Wolfgang,' Bond answered, offering him three more cigarettes which the guard promptly hid in a pocket of his uniform.

Perhaps a fly could not escape, but determined men such as those working night and day like moles, definitely could.

Bushell and the other members of the X service were concerned by the SS major's visit. Maybe it wasn't just a coincidence. Could the Germans possibly be suspecting something?

'We have to speed up the pace,' they decided.

It was now mid-March and spring was making its first appearance, with winter's rearguard struggling against the advent of the new season: on some days the skies were blue for a few hours, the sun shining, warming the prisoners' spirits and bodies before retreating again, chased away by the leaden clouds carrying with them dampness, rain and, on some nights, even snow. The snow would blanket the ground and cling to the branches of the fir trees, trapped in time, until starting to melt again when the sun re-emerged, bestowing a blinding brilliance on the white landscape.

Harry was gradually lengthening. It had now progressed beyond the outer fence and was estimated to have reached under the forest, out of the camp and beyond the no-man's zone. They had begun to dig upwards and to assemble the ladder that would lead to the exit. Now only one foot of earth remained. This was not going to be removed until the last night so as not to betray the tunnel's entrance to some chance passerby.

They now waited for the first moonless night.

• • •

Benno clasped his hands behind his head, stretched himself in his seat, straining his back hard against his chair.

On the map of the Reich opposite him, the number of pins, both yellow and red, had been multiplying with the number of enemy planes shot down since the beginning of the year.

He felt he was almost there. He had managed to locate the survivors of the two downed aircraft of that first night. One from Schnaufer's victory and two from the one that had been shot down by anti-aircraft fire. All three were in *Stalag Luft III.*

One of them had to be his man. And he was going to find out which one. Very soon.

When?

It was Friday afternoon.

He suddenly felt drained from all the exhausting work, the sleepless nights reading dozens of reports, hundreds of pages, from all the over-stimulation. Exhaustion was overwhelming him, crashing through the barrier of his endurance.

Tomorrow was Saturday. He would devote his time to preparing the documents that would authorize him to visit the *Stalag* and interrogate the prisoners. He would then forward them to Schellenberg along with his report. He would see to getting permission from the *Luftwaffe.* Maybe he would have it by Saturday night…

Sunday, then.

No, not Sunday.

Saturday night the Berlin Philharmonic was performing one of his favourite pieces, the overture from Wagner's *Götterdämmerung.* He didn't want to miss it. If he made arrangements now, he could use his contacts and get hold of a ticket, better yet, two. He would ask

Lise, that pretty blond, from the girls who worked in his section, to accompany him. He was certain she wouldn't refuse.

He smiled at the thought. Every warrior needed a break, a little diversion to regain his strength.

The *Stalag* could wait until Monday. It would still be there, with its prisoners, on Monday morning.

He spoke to Oskar through the intercom.

'Oskar, arrange for an official automobile to be made available Monday morning.'

'*Jawohl, Herr Sturmbannführer.* To where? '

'To Sagan and *Stalag Luft III*. After that, connect me with Herr Obermayer at the Philharmonic.'

CHAPTER IV

Escaping

The surface of the snow shifted, almost imperceptibly.

On the night of Friday, March 24, 1944, the winter had attempted its last assault. It began snowing at nightfall and continued for some time after that, blanketing the forest and the camp with a few inches of soft, pristine snow.

The snow stirred, sucked downward, forming a shallow hole, dark against the white. A clump of dirt was flung upwards and fell on the snow next to the hole, staining it. It could have been a mole burrowing out of its lair…

For some time, all was still.

Then something which in the dark resembled a thick, white slug poked out of the hole and remained motionless, like some strange sensor gathering data.

Then, it sank back down into the opening.

More clumps of dirt were flung across the snow since whatever was doing the digging, was doing it rapidly, widening the hole.

Within a few moments its diameter was the width of a football, and soon, even wider.

Then the digging stopped.

Absolute silence, as if the animal was eavesdropping, straining to hear the sounds of the night. But on that night, there was nothing to hear, not the slightest sound. It seemed as if even the night creatures were fast asleep in their nests.

Then, out of the opening, a hairy form appeared, rising very slowly, as if gauging the danger. It rose higher and under the hair, a face appeared which slowly swivelled around like a submarine's periscope scanning 360 degrees, seeking out potential danger.

• • •

'Go!' Bushell whispered.

Bond climbed down Harry's ladder carrying one of the small suitcases that the prisoners had made. Jenkins followed. They had been given the green light from Bushell and the escape committee to be the first to go. Priority had been determined based on several basic criteria. Foremost was the likelihood of success of the each prisoner's proposed escape plan. Those who spoke German or some other language to support their cover would be the first to leave. Bond spoke flawless German and good French, Jenkins' French was adequate. Bushell used this as the excuse to grant them priority without revealing their true identities, despite objections from some on the committee.

Before the escape, one last briefing. There was ae serious problem: the tunnel engineers had miscalculated the length of the tunnel. Its exit fell short of the cover of the forest, coming out in the no-man's zone beyond the fence, ten feet away from the safety of the trees.

It was too late for changes. They worked out an emergency plan: the first man to emerge would crawl over to the cover of the forest. He would carry a ball of string and unravel it as he made for the woods. The other end of the string would then be tied to the top rung of the ladder. From the safety of the trees, the first man out, the "control", would keep an eye on the Germans patrolling inside the fence and signal by tugging twice on the string when the coast was clear. That would be the signal that it was safe for the next man, waiting at the top of the ladder, to emerge and run for the cover of the woods.

The darkness of the moonless night was in their favour, as was the Germans' inclination to keep their attention focused on the barracks rather than beyond the fence into the no-man's zone and the forest.

In the tunnel, Bond lay down on the trolley clutching his suitcase in front of him.

The trolley began to wind its way through the tunnel on the wooden rails. Reaching the end, he got off and climbed up the ladder toward the dark exit, keeping his head down.

Seconds passed. A minute. Patience. Impatience.

A few heartbeats, a few feet to freedom!

Why the delay? What was happening?

Suddenly he felt two tugs on the string.

Without hesitation, he went up the last few rungs, emerged and without a glance back at the camp, he ran doubled over toward the trees. His boots sank into the fresh, soft snow, not yet iced over, muffling his footsteps.

He reached the trees and flung himself down next to the control, a dark shadow on the white blanket of snow.

'Everything okay?' the control asked.

'Okay!' Bond replied.

The control tugged twice on the string again

Bond stared at the opening and back at the camp. In the darkness, very little could be made out. Unless someone was staring very intently at the specific spot, nothing could be seen.

He saw the dark form of Jenkins emerge like a ghost from the bowels of the earth then running in their direction doubled over before collapsing to the ground next to them, out of breath.

'Okay?'

'Okay!'

'Let's go!'

'I'll see you in London!' the control whispered, his eyes always on the tunnel opening.

'The drinks are on me!' Bond replied.

He took out his compass with its phosphorescent indicators, held it in his palm and took a reading to get his bearings.

They began to walk through the dark trees, their boots sinking in the snow. The cold was biting, penetrating their clothing like some enemy sneaking into a defenceless town. Fortunately, the railway station at Sagan was not far, only a half mile away through the forest.

They found themselves following a narrow path that was barely noticeable in the snow in the dark, discernible only because the surface of the snow on it was level, without any bumps and dips. Bond confirmed their course with his compass and the maps the prisoners had made.

They soon reached the edge of the forest. The path ended at an asphalt road on the outskirts of the town. On the other side of the road were the first houses were visible and a little further beyond them, Bond surmised from sounds coming from that direction, the station.

He looked at his watch. A few minutes to eleven.

'Time to change!' he whispered.

They sat down on the snow, opened their suitcases, took out their civilian shoes, took off their boots and put the shoes on. They shoved their boots into the suitcases.

Bond had considered if they should risk keeping the boots. He had decided it would be better to do so, figuring they would come in handy at some point. In any event, the Germans checked identity papers, not baggage.

They examined each other to make sure they had no traces on their clothing of dirt or sand from the tunnel that might betray them.

Proceeding down the street toward the sounds of the station, they reached the entrance without incident.

Sagan was a small town, but the station was a major junction, with frequent traffic, especially on a Friday night, when it filled with soldiers going home on leave from the front.

That had been one more reason the committee had chosen a Friday night for the escape.

Trying to act normally, Bond and Jenkins entered the noisy, semi-darkened station. It was full of people, mostly soldiers, either just-arrived or waiting to board the next trains.

Bond got his bearings, spotted the ticket counter and got in the queue with Jenkins. When his turn came, he asked for two tickets to Berlin. Hearing him speaking in German, the agent didn't hesitate at all, nor did he ask for any papers. It was probably not his job to do so, nor did he have the time for it anyway, he was too busy. The travellers in the queue were impatient, anxious not to miss their connections.

He glanced at Bond indifferently, as he did with everyone, took the *Reichsmarks*, counted them out and handed him back some smaller notes and a few pfennig coins in change.

They didn't linger in the waiting room. They quickly headed for the platforms. Bond had checked from which platform the train for Berlin was leaving. The train was already there and people were boarding.

Bond and Jenkins climbed into a wagon and eventually found two seats together near an elderly German couple, most likely villagers, and a group of soldiers whose clothing stank but who were laughing and joking with each other loudly, happy to be on leave, far from the front. The train left on time, at half past eleven, for the 60-mile ride between Sagan and Berlin.

A conductor came by and asked for their tickets. No one else bothered them. A cramped trip, but so uneventful it was as if they were not travelling in the middle of the wartime Reich.

They arrived at Berlin's grand central station. The train had barely come to a stop and the doors had just opened when sirens began to howl, a hair-raising shriek, warning of an impending air raid.[39]

The crowds rushed from the platforms and waiting rooms of the station, heading for the shelters like a herd of wild animals under threat. Policemen and firemen directed them with hand gestures and whistles. Bond and Jenkins were swept along with the crowd, clinging tightly to their suitcases so as not to lose them.

Pushing and pushed, they went or rather stumbled down the concrete stairs into a shelter that seemed like the gateway to hell.

Reaching the bottom, they sat down, their backs against the cold, concrete walls, suitcases on their laps. In the dim light of the red emergency lamps on the walls, Bond saw that he was sitting next to woman of about sixty, their shoulders almost touching. To his right sat Jenkins, touching shoulders with a young mother holding her baby. All around them was a sea of faces, men, women of all ages, children, soldiers, nurses in uniform and some soldiers swathed in bandages, walking wounded on their way home from the front.

Time passed very slowly, anxiety and fear showing on the faces of everyone, beads of sweat staining many foreheads.

The muffled sounds of the first bombs could be heard, distant, like thunderclaps of a far-away storm. The bombers seemed to be targeting another area of the city that night.

------

[39]   The description of the escape is authentic, drawn from actual sources. Air raid sirens did sound out sometime after midnight resulting in the lights going out in the camp and the tunnel, stopping the flow of escaping prisoners while it lasted.

Inside the shelter not a sound was heard, not even a whisper, a silence so deep it seemed like a scream. Bond recognised it as the sound of agony and fear.

Suddenly a cluster of bombs landed nearby, perhaps from a bomber which had made a slight error in targeting. The whole shelter shuddered as if shaken by some mythical subterranean beast trying to break through the earth's crust to escape to the surface above. The lights flickered and went out, plunging the shelter into blackness so absolute it seemed as if they were buried in the bowels of the earth.

The baby in the arms of the woman next to Jenkins began to cry, shattering the silence. Another baby in the crowd took up the refrain. As if the babies' cries were a signal, many of the little children in the shelter began to wail also, turning the silence into a cacophony of sounds. What irony, Bond thought, if it were all to end with a British bomb. Would the shelter be able to withstand a direct hit?

Bond felt a trembling hand seeking his own, squeezing it tightly in fruitless hope of comfort.

The lights flickered and finally came back on. The elderly woman pulled her hand away as if ashamed and cried out in a whisper:

'*Verdammte Engländer!*[40]

Then, embarrassed by her outburst she added apologetically, 'I lost my husband in an air raid two months ago.'

'*Es tut mir wirklich leid,*[41] Bond responded.

The baby continued crying.

---

[40]   "Damned English!"
[41]   "I'm truly sorry."

'Don't be afraid, my treasure,' the mother whispered in her ear, rocking her gently in her arms. But the baby wouldn't stop. The young woman opened her blouse, brought her baby's face closer and offered her breast. The infant sought out the nipple and began suckling, finally content.

The woman's eyes met Bond's. He smiled at her. She returned a fleeting smile of her own.

A few more moments passed, seeming like hours. No more bombs fell nearby. The sirens finally sounded the all clear. The crowd stirred and began to head for the stairs leading out of the shelter.

Bond and Jenkins reached the surface out on the street where the crowd quickly dispersed. A little further down a building was ablaze, probably struck by the bombs that had shaken the shelter. The light of the fire somewhat brightened the area around them.

Many buildings were destroyed, roofs collapsed, the walls that remained looking like the few teeth left in a rotting mouth. Shells of buildings, with piles of rubble both inside and spilling out onto the pavement, rubble of bricks, stone, wooden beams, mortar. The mounds of rubble from the more recent strikes extended well into the streets, not yet cleared by the clean-up crews.

The streets were pockmarked with craters, some filled up with the plentiful rubble available, others more recent, still gaping.

Bond had lived through the bombings of London in September and October of 1940. The destruction then paled in comparison with what he was seeing now.

As if by some miracle, amidst the shattered ruins, there were some buildings that had survived barely scathed, only their windows broken. Boards and heavy paper served to replace the glass.

They headed back to the railway station. Bond queued up for their tickets. When his turn came he asked for two first-class tickets for the express train to Munich. Paying, he took the tickets and his change and went back to Jenkins who was seated on a bench in the waiting room guarding their suitcases. Bond nodded slightly, indicating that all was still okay. Obviously, the escape had not yet been discovered.

They waited in silence on the bench, watching the crowds coming and going around them and glancing frequently at the station clock high on the wall opposite them. The seconds seemed like minutes, the minutes like hours, endless hours, as if time had come to a standstill.

But it hadn't. The Berlin-Hamburg-Frankfurt- Munich express was on time. Bond and Jenkins rose, and went out onto the platform, walking alongside the train amid the disembarking passengers until they spotted a first class car marked for Munich. They climbed aboard, made their way down the corridor and entered the first empty compartment. They placed their suitcases on the racks above and sat down, Jenkins by the window, Bond next to him.

Jenkins looked out the window at the darkened tracks. He could make out a line of shadowy forms walking along the tracks. They stopped and began to work with pickaxes and shovels. Jenkins watched silently, sullen, looking but not seeing, his eyes focused inwardly on his own thoughts.

'I know,' Bond said to him quietly. 'It's difficult to see them as the enemy right now.'

Jenkins didn't respond.

Suddenly one of the figures stumbled, dropped its shovel. Another shadowy figure, a different shaped silhouette, lifted something in his hand and brought it down with force on the first, once, then again and again. The scene was all the more nightmarish because there was no sound behind the window. Bond realised that they were probably watching Russian POW's working on the tracks and their guards, SS, most likely.

'That's what we are fighting against,' Jenkins whispered.

The door to the compartment opened.

'*Ist hier noch ein Platz frei?*[42] the general asked.

'*Aber selbstverständlich, Herr Generalmajor,*[43] Bond replied.

The general entered, holding a briefcase and a suitcase. Bond got up and helped him place the suitcase in the baggage rack. The general thanked him and sat down opposite Jenkins. He took a newspaper out of his briefcase.

A little later, the door opened again and a middle-aged woman came in. With her old-fashioned but expensive dress, lace-trimmed on the collar and cuffs, her three-strand pearl necklace, the diamonds on her fingers, she was obviously a woman of the Prussian aristocracy. She had probably been forced to flee from her estates in East Prussia due to the latest advances by the Russian forces and was most likely now on her way to join relatives in Munich.

Bond gallantly rose again and lifted her two large suitcases onto the baggage rack. He received a curt thank you in return for his effort. She sat down next to the general.

A small lurch.

Right on time, at four thirty on the dot, the train started off.

---

[42]   "Is there a free place here?"
[43]   "Of course, Major General!"

The first hour passed by silently with the general reading his newspaper, the woman reading a book, Jenkins staring out into the darkness and Bond cat-napping with his eyes half-shut.

Finally the general folded his newspaper. A long, dull journey he had done so many times!

Bond sitting across from him caught his bored glance and smiled at him. 'May I ask you something?'

'Please.'

'Where did you win the Oak Leaves on your Iron Cross?'

'Ah, these. At the retaking of Kharkov.'[44]

'A great victory for von Manstein,' Bond commented. 'How are things now?'

'The front has stabilized from the Baltic down through the Ukraine to the Black Sea.'

'We are French airplane engineers,' Bond said in introduction. 'We are working at the Focke-Wulf factory in Erfurt. Professor Tank[45] paid us the honour of including us in his team designing the

---

[44] *Eichenlaub zum Ritterkreuz des Eisernen Kreuzes*: Oak Leaves on the Cross of the Knight of the Iron Cross. The first of the top medals of the Reich. Above that was the *Schwerter* (swords) and then the *Brillianten* (diamonds). In February-March of 1943, after the Fall of Stalingrad, Field Marshall von Manstein's lightening counterstrike crushed the Soviet advance and stabilized the front.

[45] Karl Tank: chief designer of fighters at Focke-Wulf. After the success of the Focke-Wulf 190, he was honoured by having the consequent fighters assigned the letters "Ta" (after Tank) as the identifier. Aside from the 154A, he also designed the high-performance single-engine, single-seat high-altitude pursuit fighter, the Ta-152H. Active units began to receive this plane in the final weeks of the war.

new night fighter. We were in Berlin for a meeting with engineers of the *Luftwaffe*.'

'You speak excellent German. Have you been in Germany a long time?'

'*Qu'est ce qu'il dit?*[46] Jenkins asked loudly, playing up his role.

'*Je t'expliquerai plus tard mon vieux !*[47] Bond said to him in a loud voice and then turned to the general again.

'He was recently deafened by a bomb explosion in the factory. Before the war we were employed by the *Societé Nationale des Constructions Aéronautiques*, which you may know as the *Devoitine*, at their Toulouse Blagnac factory. When the Minister of Production, M. Bichelonne[48] signed the agreement with Herr Speer to allow Frenchmen to work in Germany, we grabbed at the opportunity. Salaries are much higher here. But I had learned my German in school and perfected it on my vacations to your country. We are on our way back now after two weeks' sick leave.'

'And what are you designing with the Professor now?' the general asked, clearly very interested.

Bond leaned forward, almost conspiratorially. 'A new night fighter. One of the new weapons that will turn the tide of war back

---

[46]   'What is he saying?'

[47]   'll explain later, mate'

[48]   A minister in Petain's Vichy government. Albert Speer, an architect, had taken over the Ministry of Production in Germany in 1943 and despite the bombing campaign, had managed to triple production in 1944. He was the only one to admit his culpability at the Nuremberg Trials where he was sentenced to 20 years in prison. His autobiography "Inside the Third Reich" was very successful and remains one of the "classic" works on the Second World War.

in our favour,' he said, emphasising the "our". 'The Focke-Wulf Ta-154a. A revolutionary plane!'

'How so?'

'General, first, because it is constructed of wood like the English Mosquito. That way we conserve precious raw materials, aluminium, steel, etc. for use elsewhere. A high wing, two engines, Jumo 213A's, 1776 horsepower each. Electronic equipment, the FuG 202 BC-1 Liechtenstein. Two 30mm cannon, the MK-108, General, and two 20mm MG-151 in the nose, capable of downing any enemy bomber with one volley. Top speed 640 kilometres per hour at an altitude of 8,500 metres.' Bond said, feigning excitement. 'Fast enough to outfly th0se Mosquitoes which cause us such problems!'

'Sounds excellent! And when will this marvel be ready?'

'The prototype already flew successfully in November. Unofficially we have named it Moskito. We have a joke among ourselves, General: it takes a mosquito to catch a mosquito!'

The general laughed. From being dull this trip had become quite interesting, thanks to his very likable and clever French travelling companion.

'And when does mass production begin?'

Bond's expression turned serious.

'We have a slight problem. The wood glue…it has not yet been perfected and the parts come unstuck. They are very sensitive to humidity….'[49]

---

49 This and other production problems resulted in the delivery of just a few Moskitos to active units in the final weeks of the war.

The general raised his eyebrows, surprised that such an accomplishment would be delayed by such a humble material as wood glue.

'I'm sure you will resolve the issue soon enough. What does your aircraft look like?'

'If I had some paper I can show you,' Bond replied.

'That's easily resolved!' the general said as he opened his briefcase and took out a sheet of paper. He gave it along with a pencil to Bond who began to make a sketch.

At that moment, the door to compartment opened.

'Your papers!' a policeman ordered.

The general and the woman handed theirs over first. The policeman glanced at the papers quickly and returned them.

Bond handed him his identity cards, his leave booklet and all other necessary travel documents, all correctly endorsed with appropriate stamps, dates, etc., thanks to the camp's talented forgery service.[50] Feigning indifference, he resumed sketching. The policeman took the documents, scrutinising each one very carefully, looking back and forth between each document and Bond.

The general finally exploded.

'*Ach, beeilen Sie sich doch! Sehen Sie nicht daß wir beschäftig sind!*'[51]

---

[50]   The Reich was especially bureaucratic. Citizens had two identity cards, the *Kennkarte* and the *Ausweiss* or *vorläufiges Ausweis* (permanent or temporary version). Soldiers carried the *Soldbuch* (paybook). Foreigners were required to carry in addition, what Bond showed: the *Polizeiliche Bescheinigung, Urlaubsschein, Rückerschein* and the *Sonderpaß*.

[51]   "Hurry up, already! Can't you see we're busy?"

The policeman was taken aback by the general's tone. With the inborn respect of the German for his superiors, he obeyed immediately and returned all Bond's documents to him. He took Jenkins' papers, took a quick look at the photographs and returned them to him as well.

As if to appease the general, he murmured '*Gute Reise!*'[52] and left, closing the door behind him.

'*Dummkopf!*'[53] the general muttered. 'They see spies everywhere…'

'Do you think they thought you were an English spy, general?'

The general was dumbstruck for a moment until he finally digested his companion's witticism.

Grasping the Frenchman's humour, he burst out laughing. 'That's excellent! Very good! I must tell that to my friends!'

Bond handed him the sketch.

The woman looked up, her nose in the air. She didn't deign to join in the conversation with these rather ill-dressed men, even though the younger of the two was definitely not at all bad-looking, not even with the general who, judging from his accent was from Bavaria and thus an inferior.

'The army too is preparing its own ace,' the general said. 'A new super weapon, the *Königstiger*. Have you heard of it?'

'I confess, no, I have not. Why super weapon?'

'Sixty-five tons! Sloping frontal armour, maximum thickness at the glacis plate and the front of the turret, 200mm, making it impervious to any known tank gun or anti-armour weapon of the

---

52   "Good journey"
53   "Imbecile!"

enemy under battle conditions! Suspension like on the Tiger and Panther, but with nine wheels on each side instead of eight. And the gun? The new 88mm, the L71. It can penetrate any enemy armour at 1000 metres!'[54]

Not to be shown up, the general took the pencil and paper from Bond and quickly sketched the tank.

'With all these new weapons we will finally win the war, even if it's at the last hour,' the general concluded. 'We must outlast them for a few months more, until these weapons reach the front in numbers, fully operational. And who knows? If the Allies land in France and we throw them back into the sea, perhaps their policy will change and they will revise their demand for unconditional surrender. Unconditional surrender! Unheard of, an insult! They didn't demand that even during the first war. Maybe then they will see that the real danger in this world is the communists whom they support so much. Do you know that, though their tanks and guns on the Eastern Front are Russian, their automobiles and most of their other materials are American or British?'

'No, general, I didn't know that.' Bond said, though he was well aware of that fact.

---

[54] Called the King Tiger by the Allies. The glacis is the "bonnet" of a tank. With regard to the tank's gun, the L stood for *Länge* (length) indicating the ratio of the barrel's length to its diameter, i.e. 6,248mm. In action, the *Königstiger* proved difficult to manage and not very maneuverable, but virtually invulnerable to Allied tank guns and anti-tank weapons. The Americans first encountered this tank in 1944, in the Battle of the Ardennes. Some 500 were produced.

The new day was dawning. The train arrived at the station in Hannover, where it remained for half an hour, as its wagons were detached and attached to other trains heading either northward to Hamburg and Kiel or south to Frankfurt and Munich. It occurred to Bond that in spite of the bombings, the German rail system still worked effectively. A piece of intelligence that would interest C, as much as the "titbit" about the new panzer unwittingly offered up by the general.

They went up to the dining car and bought sandwiches with sausage and coffee, ersatz[55] of course, awful stuff. Bond could still not get used to it.

With a slight jerk the train started up again.

The conversation with the general moved on to other things, as if they were old friends. They spoke of vacations before the war in the south of France, skiing in the Alps, the merits of a Château Lafite compared to those of a Romanée Conti.[56] As an old aristocrat, the general knew how to enjoy the simple pleasures of life. They even spoke of the many obvious as well as hidden attractions of Paris.

'General, I must confess that the first time I went with a woman was when I was 16, at 5, rue du Nord, on my first visit to Paris,' Bond said, referring to an actual experience of his.

'Ah, Paris! The Folies Bergère!' the general sighed. The aristocratic Prussian lady, eavesdropping on their conversation, suddenly gave

---

[55]   Substitute. Because of the Allied naval blockade, goods from abroad, coffee, cocoa, chocolate, tea, etc., could not be imported. As a result, substitutes were created from other raw materials.

[56]   Two of the finest wines of France, the first a Bordeaux, the other a Burgundy.

them a disapproving look. Men were all simply too vulgar, wherever they were from.

'We've beaten them easily at war,' the general mused, 'but the French are our masters when it comes to pleasure!'

It was past noon when the train pulled into Munich. Bond was sure that by now the escape would have been discovered as those who had made it out would be missing from the morning roll call. How would the Germans react? What emergency measures would they take? If so, what awaited them?

The train rolled to a stop. Bond helped the Prussian woman get her suitcases off the train to the platform where she was met. She thanked him, not quite as coldly as before. This young Frenchman after all did have some manners…

Together with the general, they entered the main concourse of the terminal, full of people, soldiers on leave reuniting with their families and loved ones, with embraces and kisses, citizens, both German and foreign.

Bond quickly spotted pairs of uniformed policemen, as well as others, Gestapo most likely, characteristically attired in their black leather coats and black hats, stopping people at random, demanding to see their identification papers.

He and Jenkins stuck close to the general. No one would think of stopping two gentlemen accompanying a highly decorated general.

They reached the exit.

'Will you be staying in Munich?' the general asked.

'Yes, General. We plan to rest for a day and see the sights before continuing on to Freiburg and then Lyon.'

'Then I recommend the Hotel Bayernischer Hof on the Promenadenplatz. A little expensive, but very good. Tell the concierge you were sent by me, Jürgen, *Freiherr* von Himmelstein.'[57]

'Thank you, General. I'm Michel Gary.' Bond introduced himself with the name on his documents. 'And Paul Duval,' he added, indicating Jenkins.

'Enjoy your stay. *Auf Wiedersehen!*'[58] They exchanged farewells.

It was a bright, sunny day, their first day of freedom, as if they had left winter behind in Sagan and were being welcomed by spring.

'Let's follow the general's advice,' Bond said.

He knew that they needed a day's rest and a good night's sleep which had not been possible on the train. He felt a good hotel would provide the best refuge. The Germans would be searching trains, stations, the streets for the escaped POW's, not the luxury hotels and certainly not one in faraway Munich. For that matter, it would not be easy for them to locate two foreign workers among the six million circulating in the Reich.

They walked to the hotel. At the reception, Bond asked for a room, mentioning that the hotel had been recommended by General von Himmelstein.

'Ah! Has the general returned?' the receptionist asked.

'We travelled together on the train from Berlin,' Bond replied.

'Wonderful! I hope we will see him soon in our restaurant. Your identification, please…a formality, of course, since you were recommended by the general…regulations, you know…'

---

[57]   *"Freiherr"*: a baron. Himmelstein: Heavenly Stone

[58]   "Until we meet again." Bond encountered the general again in "The Caves of Odin".

'I understand completely,' Bond smiled and handed over their identity cards.

The receptionist just gave them a cursory glance.

'Please sign here.' He turned the guestbook around toward Bond and pointed to where he had written their names.

'Your key.'

In the room, Jenkins let out a loud sigh of relief. 'Bond, you gave me the fright of my life on that train. I thought you were overdoing it a little with the general!'

'A calculated risk! I followed the example of a trick from Poe.'

'What does Poe have to do with this?'

'I remembered one of his stories - I forget the title - that had made an impression on me. The hero had an important document in his possession that some people were after. He had to hide it in his office that he knew would be searched. So what did he do? He crumpled it up and left it right there on his desk. The people tore the office apart looking for it but no one thought to check the crumpled paper on the desk. Just like us: the Germans are searching for escaped prisoners. Fugitives hide and try to avoid attracting attention. They don't start a conversation with generals in first class on a train. We are so visible that we have become invisible!'

'I didn't know that American literature was on the MI6 syllabus!'

'It isn't. But you can't imagine what one learns at Eton!'

Bond told Jenkins to get some rest while he went out to do some shopping.

He returned some time later, his arms full. He opened up his packages: a change of underwear, a fresh shirt, a new jacket for each of them as well as a few other items.

They bathed, shaved, put on their new clothes and went down to the restaurant with its bright chandeliers and shining mirrors on the walls. The *maitre d'*, a tall, slender, gracious, white-haired man, led them to a table in the luxurious dining room with its velvet chairs, original paintings on the walls, and crystal chandeliers. White linen tablecloths with silver cutlery, crystal glassware and porcelain dinnerware, most likely Meissen,[59] elegantly adorned the tables.

The *maitre d'* handed them menus, while commenting apologetically in French, 'Unfortunately, our menu is not as it was… the war, you know…'

It seemed that he had been informed by the concierge that they were Frenchmen and had been introduced by the general. They chose a schnitzel with carrots and potatoes, and a cabbage salad.

'Our wine cellar however is still well-stocked' the *maitre d'* said. 'Fortunately, our relations with our suppliers have remained intact…'

And so they had. Bond selected a Nuits-Saint-Georges 1939.

The schnitzels may not have been an inspired choice, but they were well-prepared and filling and the wine was up to expectations. The dining room was filled with well-dressed men and women in civilian clothing along with a scattering of high-ranking officers in uniform. It was Saturday evening and the Bavarians were not about to let the war interfere with their pleasures.

They completed their meal with apple strudel and whipped cream, real, not ersatz. The *maitre d'* inquired in French if everything

---

59   The hotel was bombed and destroyed on the night of April 24, 1944. It reopened after the war. Under its ruins, the famous *Spiegelsaal* (the hall of mirrors) was found virtually intact.

had been to their satisfaction and confided nostalgically that before the war he had worked in Deauville.[60] Bond thanked him and left a good tip.

When they had returned to the room, Jenkins asked him, 'Tell me, what you told the general about their fighter, was it true?'

'Absolutely! There are foreign workers in all German factories. And some among them are our eyes and ears. But what the general told us about the new panzer, that, I think, is news.'

Bond laid out the silk map of Germany on his bed and looked at it again. They had studied alternate routes to take from Munich. Bond had rejected the shortest route, directly south to Switzerland, because the Alps and the Zugspitze stood in the way, impassable at this time of year because of the snow. Another route was southeast to the banks of Lake Constance or, as it was called in German, the Bodensee. The Rhine began from its western end. But then to cross over into Switzerland, they would have to find a boat. Not easy. The Germans would surely be patrolling it very closely.

That left the eastern route, through Austria. The main advantage of this route as far as Bond was concerned, was that he knew the region well from skiing trips in the winter and mountain-climbing vacations in the summer.

And he knew of yet one more advantage that just might give them the decisive edge.

• • •

---

[60] A spa on the coast of Normandy.

Benno had earlier forwarded to the camp commandant the approval from his superiors for his visit to *Stalag Luft III*, announcing that he would be arriving on Monday. He now had Oskar telephone the camp and confirm that the message had been received.

A short while later, Oskar knocked on his door.

'Come in,' Benno said.

Oskar appeared quite upset, a highly unusual state for him.

'Something has happened, *Herr Sturmbannführer.* They said on the telephone…they were extremely upset, almost incoherent…a prison break took place during the night!'

'What!?'

Benno sprang to his feet, feeling a tight feeling of unease in his gut. He made a quick decision.

'Find me a car, Oskar! Right now! We're leaving immediately!'

They arrived at the camp at eleven only to be greeted by complete chaos. There was no one to receive them at the Administration Building, s not even a guard to open his car door as would normally be the case.

Inside, there were only soldiers and non-coms shouting into telephones. Benno learned from one of them that all the officers were inside the camp.

Benno and Oskar practically ran to the camp's entrance demanding that the guards allow them in. Benno's attitude, the tone of his voice and his uniform were fortunately enough to grant them entrance as the valid authorization they had was for Monday, not for this day, Saturday, two days earlier.

He arrived at the parade ground where the prisoners were still assembled, armed guards surrounding them and the officers up front.

Benno spotted the commandant, von Lindeiner.[61] Approaching him, he announced without ceremony who he was and demanded to know what had happened.

The commandant was as pale as if he had seen a ghost or rather, as if he himself was a ghost dressed in the uniform of a *Luftwaffe* colonel. He said in a choked voice that they had discovered a tunnel through which some prisoners had escaped.

'How many? Who were they?' Benno demanded to know.

The commandant swallowed hard. He didn't have any answers to either question. Between 50 and 100. They were taking a roll call of all the prisoners now to determine who was missing but with over a 1000 of them it was a time-consuming process.

Fifty to 100! Benno couldn't believe his ears. Were these *Luftwaffe* people totally incompetent? He returned to the Administration Building and demanded to be connected with Schellenberg's office. When the call finally came through, he asked to speak to the *Brigadeführer* urgently: What? He was not there? On a Saturday? He was at home?

He hung up and called Schellenberg's home. He had the number for emergencies and this certainly was the case.

A woman's voice answered. His wife. Yes, it was urgent he speak to her husband immediately.

'Benno, what's going on?' he heard Schellenberg ask.

He briefed him quickly.

---

[61] Von Lindeiner acted very correctly towards the prisoners. After the escape, he retired to his estate, not far from Sagan. He eventually returned to active duty, fought against the Russians and survived the war.

Schellenberg was silent for a moment before replying.

'You did well to inform me. Stay there as long as necessary and call me when you have any news.'

Benno hung up. He was sure that Schellenberg would inform Himmler immediately and he in turn would rush to inform Hitler. One more nail in Göring's coffin.

But he himself had a very uneasy feeling: that among the men who had escaped would be his prime candidate, Squadron Leader Rodger.[62]

---

[62]   Seventy-six prisoners escaped, including a Greek pilot in the RAF. Three (two Norwegians and one Dutchman) reached England. The rest were all apprehended and 50 of them, including Bushell, were executed by order of an enraged Hitler. After the war, many of those guilty of the executions were themselves tried, convicted and executed.

CHAPTER V

Running

Bond slept well and awoke refreshed. He and Jenkins washed up and went down to the dining room for breakfast: Coffee, ersatz of course, milk, bread and buns (freshly-baked from the restaurant's own bakery – and delicious), omelette and sausages.

The returned to their room for their suitcases and came back down.

Bond paid the bill, leaving a generous tip (since they had been introduced by their friend, the general). At the hotel entrance, the porter handed them two additional purchases Bond had made the day before - bicycles. They lashed their suitcases to the bicycles' rear racks, shouldered their knapsacks and after handing the porter his obligatory tip, rode off, following his directions out of the city.

Sunday was a gloomy, overcast day threatening rain, as if Providence, like a fickle woman always changing moods and behaviour, was now showing her dour side after yesterday's bright and sunny disposition.

They cycled down Munich's wide boulevards amid the pedestrians, the mass transit vehicles, many bicycles and just a few automobiles, mostly military. It was obvious that petrol-rationing had limited the circulation of privately-owned vehicles.

They reached the southern outskirts of the city without incident and took the road in the direction of the Chiemsee. A few kilometres out of the city, they left the main road and continued travelling on side roads that wound through fields, forests, farms and small villages. This route was much safer and more suited to their cover as two Frenchmen who were taking advantage of the opportunity to do some sightseeing in Bavaria before returning to their homeland.

A light rain began to fall, not heavy but persistent, one likely to last for hours, perhaps all day, soon soaking through their clothing and finally mingling with their perspiration.

After the first hour, Jenkins began to fall behind. He was twenty years older than Bond, not in very good shape and the three months' incarceration in the *Stalag* had taken its toll.

After another hour had passed, Bond decided it was time for a break. Up until then, they had encountered little traffic since leaving Munich. The main street of the first village they had passed through was almost deserted, the few people circulating barely noticing them, in a hurry to get out of the rain. At least the rain was serving in their favour. It seemed that, as it was Sunday, the local inhabitants were either in church for Sunday Mass, since most Bavarians were Catholic, or frequenting the cafés and *Bierstuben* in their villages.

Bond found a spot in the woods off the road, in a grove of tall evergreens, the kind the Germans referred to as *Fichten*, a cross between pine and fir, which offered them some protection from the rain. Bond untied the empty suitcases which were now just excess weight. They could not leave them behind at the hotel because that would have aroused suspicion. Looking around, Bond found a dense clump of ferns nearby under which he hid the two cases. He stepped back to make sure they were not visible from the path that led into the grove from the road.

They sat down, leaning against two trees. The ground was thickly carpeted in pine needles that had kept it dry.

Bond unfolded his map and studied it for a while, estimating their current position. He figured they had covered somewhere between 15 and 20 kilometres since leaving the city. He took out his compass and took a reading to orient himself.

They drank a little water and rested for half an hour. Bond knew that any longer and their rhythm would be affected.

'Should we be off, then?'

Jenkins rose and went to his bicycle.

It was almost noon and still raining. They were on the main road approaching the third village when Bond spotted a roadblock up ahead.

It wasn't anything official, just a *Landwehr* man and two *Hitlerjugend* boys with ancient rifles slung over their shoulders, standing by the side of the road that led into the village.

It was too late to turn back. That would have definitely looked suspicious.

Bond continued cycling, approached them and came to a stop even before the *Landwehr* man could say, 'Halt!'

'Good day!' Bond greeted them with a disarming smile. 'Is this the right way to the Chiemsee? General von Himmelstein suggested we follow these charming country roads rather than the central highway but it's so easy to get lost!'

The old soldier was surprised by the question, the cyclist's slightly accented German – and the name of the general. He didn't recognise the name but, after all, a general is a general!

He responded, giving directions and pointing.

'Thank you,' Bond responded. 'Is there a bakery open today?'

'Yes, a little further down. It's open for a few hours on Sunday.'

Suddenly, he remembered his duty and asked for their papers.

Bond handed him his identity card which the soldier examined, studying the photograph and the validity date, all in order.

'Do you need anything more?' Bond offered helpfully.

'That won't be necessary,' the soldier replied. 'Just the other man's…'

Jenkins, silent but trying to imitate the carefree attitude of Bond's casual traveller, handed the soldier his identity cards as well. The soldier glanced at it and returned it.

'Are you French?' he asked.

'French airplane engineers working for Focke-Wulf. We're on leave and thought we would do some sightseeing before going back,' Bond replied smoothly.

'Have a pleasant journey,' the old soldier said.

He had fought at Verdun in 1916 and had learned to respect the French. '*Au revoir*,' he added, dusting off the little bit of French he remembered.

'*Merci, Auf Wiedersehen*,' Bond responded as they set off.

The soldier and the two boys watched them cycle down the main street, stopping 300 metres away in front of the bakery he had recommended.

'Were they really French, Herr Taufer?' one of the boys asked.

'Of course, Willy,' the soldier answered. 'French…they reminded me of younger days…remind me to tell you a story about Verdun when we get back.'

He considered the urgent message they had received earlier that had required him to stand in the rain with the two boys instead of allowing him to enjoy his Sunday in the warmth of his own home and then later, the company of his friends in the only *Bierstube* in the village. The message referred to a mass escape from a *Stalag* by British airmen. But these two strangers were anything but British airmen. Their papers were in order. They seemed easy-going, not at all in any hurry nor appearing anxious. Perhaps a little strange, going to the Chiemsee at this time of year, but then again, why not? The lake always attracted both German and foreign visitors. He recalled those pre-war days with nostalgia. Even now, in the spring, many tourists from Munich made the trip just to get away from the city for a few days.

Anyway, who ever heard of fugitives, in the middle of the day, casually going about with bicycles and knapsacks, asking for directions? The older man, around fiftyish and much too thin, certainly didn't look like an RAF officer. And if they were escaped prisoners, wouldn't they be travelling south, to Switzerland, rather than east?

Bond stepped into the bakery which was also a small grocery shop and bought a loaf of bread, cheese and a sausage with his food ration card. He paid, climbed back on his bicycle, which Jenkins had been holding for him, and they continued on their way out of the village. An hour later, they got off the road and sought shelter under a small grove of trees with a dense canopy of leaves. Finding a fairly dry spot, they dismounted from their bicycles and sat down to enjoy their lunch, the supplies Bond had bought at the bakery.

'Picnic in the forest in the rain,' Jenkins commented. 'Just like home!' He looked at Bond as he chewed. 'Do you think we'll make it?'

'Why not?' Bond replied, trying to sound more encouraging than he actually felt. 'We've made it this far. We've had two days of freedom already.'

He considered their strategy from this point on. Until now they had been especially lucky, they had survived three security checks, on the train, in the station and now in the village. But they wouldn't always be so lucky, nor have a general as an unwitting partner. At the next checkpoint, they might be more suspicious, less trusting, more thorough. Maybe it was time to move on to the next phase of the plan, to become invisible, avoiding villages and all encounters, travelling while maintaining as low a profile as possible, even moving only at night if necessary. It would take longer, but their safety was a priority.

They resumed their journey after Bond consulted his map and compass. This time they followed trails and unpaved country roads turned to mud by the rain. They were forced to travel slowly with a good deal of exertion, splashing through puddles, the muddy water staining their shoes and trousers, at times dismounting to bypass on foot what appeared to be deep gullies full of water. They were soaked to the bone and drenched in sweat. Glancing behind him, Bond noticed the professor gasping for breath.

They were moving slowly, at a walker's pace, Bond stopping every so often to get his bearings whenever visibility permitted. The combination of the rain and the fact that it was Sunday had turned the countryside into a deserted landscape. They avoided any village, even the smallest, even the occasional farmhouse. Smoke rose from some of the chimneys, barely discernible against the grey sky. When they heard dogs barking they were forced to circle around, through fields and woods, sometimes following a fence until there was an opening, stretching out the distances they had to cover, changing direction so frequently that, without Bond's compass, they would have become completely disoriented especially since there was no sun to rely on.

It was well into the afternoon when they entered a large forest. Bond now felt a little safer. Here, they were less likely to encounter anyone, except possibly a woodcutter. At times cycling along the trail, at other times on foot, they continued on their way.

Suddenly, deep in the thick forest, they came upon the wreckage of an airplane. As they approached, Bond recognised it as a B-17 of the 8th Army Air Force.[63] Both wings had been sheared off the

---

63 8th USAAF, Eighth Bomber Command of the American Army Air Force. It flew B-17 Flying Fortress and B-24 Liberator four-engine bombers. The American strategy was precision daylight bombing strikes on specific targets (factories, etc). The bombers had strong defensive armaments (12-13 12.5mm machine guns) against German fighters and an advanced bombsight, the Norden, to locate their target. In effect, though, on many missions only a small number of bombs hit the intended targets and losses suffered from German fighter aircraft were prohibitive. This changed dramatically when in February 1944, the P-51 Mustang fighter plane made its appearance with a range long enough to supply cover for the bombers all the way into Germany and back. That was when the Allies finally secured control of the skies over Europe, a prerequisite for the invasion at Normandy.

fuselage, one had even lost its engines, which were scattered a few feet away, the propellers bent. The fuselage was broken in two, the front portion so crushed it was barely recognisable, as if it were a toy twisted out of shape by the hands of some giant. The rear portion however was almost intact. From the amount of rust that was visible, Bond figured it had been there for several months. Some treetops had been sheared off from the crash as if by a huge saw, and lay scattered around the site.

Bond entered the plane. The Germans had ripped out whatever was usable. But at least it was dry inside. He gestured to Jenkins to follow him in, leaving the bicycles outside. They made themselves comfortable. From his knapsack, Bond took out a bottle of schnapps, another of his Munich purchases, drank some and handed the bottle to Jenkins.

Bond felt the liquid warming his insides. He opened up his map again.

'We're going to have to find shelter for the night. Do you think you can keep going for a while longer?'

Jenkins nodded his assent, even though he was exhausted.

After resting for half an hour, they set off once again.

Two hours later dusk was upon them and Bond searched anxiously for suitable shelter for the night, without any success. Finally, Providence, which had been testing them all day long, smiled on them once more. In a small clearing they spotted a woodcutter's cabin. Leaving Jenkins under the cover of the trees with the bicycles, Bond cautiously approached the cabin to check it out.

There was no one about. He tried the door, it was unlocked.

The cabin was empty except for a ring of stones, forming a small cooking area directly under the chimney. There were no sign of ashes, an indication that it had not been used for some time.

An ideal hideout. Isolated and dry.

Bond went back to get Jenkins and the bicycles and they returned to the cabin. Once inside, they took off their sodden jackets and changed into the clothing that had been altered from uniforms by the camp's tailoring service.

'I'll go fetch some firewood,' Bond said.

He went out and gathered whatever dry branches he could find and dug around for dry pine needles to act as kindling. Just like the boy scouts, he thought to himself with a smile.

Back in the cabin, he took out J's lighter and using some of the paper their lunch had been wrapped in, he lit the kindling. He blew on it to strengthen the flame. Eventually, the damp wood grudgingly caught fire, crackling and smoking. In a while the fire was burning properly and the area gradually warmed. They hung up their wet clothing on hooks that the woodcutters had pounded into a beam almost directly over the fire for that very purpose. Bond took off his shoes and socks, putting on dry socks from his knapsack as well as his RAF boots, wonderfully warmer with their lining than those civilian shoes. Jenkins followed suit.

They ate the remaining bread, sausage and cheese along with two tins of corned beef, courtesy of the Red Cross, that they had brought with them from the camp. They finished off the meal with a little chocolate and a shot of schnapps. This time Bond was more sparing because he wasn't sure when he could replenish it. It was meant as a restorative, not a pleasure. They drank a little water from their canteens, yet another of Bond's Munich purchases. Up until now, water hadn't been a problem, as they had topped off their canteens from a fountain in the village.

The fire would stay lit for about three hours, based on the amount of wood Bond had gathered, long enough for the place to stay warm and dry their clothing.

'You know, Bond,' Jenkins said suddenly. "My damned pride is to blame for all of this. It was foolish of me to go on that flight…and now I've gotten you involved…'

He felt a need to explain himself, to apologise, even though Bond hadn't asked or said a word.

'There were many who doubted our project, what we had accomplished. They considered us a bunch of crazy scientists…you know they call us boffins, wasting time and money better spent elsewhere. But we believed in our project, it was extremely important. What scientist doesn't feel that way about his work? That's why I wanted to prove how the H2S when used correctly would perform as promised. Foolish pride perhaps…'

He looked at Bond, and took another bite of food.

'And indeed it did perform as promised,' Bond said. 'As we saw for ourselves in Berlin.'

'Do you think it was worth it?'

'I think what you did took a lot of courage,' Bond responded. 'I believe anyone who puts his life at risk for what he believes in is worthy of respect. Now let's get some sleep. We'll need all our strength tomorrow.'

Using their knapsacks as pillows, they lay down on the wooden floor of the cabin on either side of the fire.

Bond awoke first, a little stiff but rested. Through the gap under the front door he could see the first signs of daylight. He stepped outside, leaving Jenkins still asleep. He looked at his watch. It was half past six.

The rain had stopped. Through the treetops he could make out what seemed to be a clear sky. He opened up his map and studied it. He estimated that they had covered two thirds of the distance to the west bank of the lake, some 50 kilometres as the crow flies.

They shared a tin of corned beef and one of milk for breakfast. Before they left, Bond buried the empty tins a distance from the cabin to avoid detection if by some remote chance, someone were to happen by. The ashes left behind were not likely to raise any suspicion as any woodcutter could have lit a fire.

Sometimes cycling, at other times on foot again, pushing their bicycles through the underbrush when one trail ended until they could find a new one, after about an hour, they finally came to the edge of the forest. From behind the cover of the last trees, Bond scrutinised the terrain.

Fields, scattered farmhouses, dirt roads, clusters of trees, the houses of a small community.

Blue sky and sunshine. The rain and sun had melted away the last of the snow but there was a lot of mud and puddles of water everywhere.

It was Monday and the farmers were in their fields. He could see several small herds of cows grazing in fenced-in fields and in others, further away, some people. A peaceful scene, far from the bombings, the ruins, the war.

It would not be easy to pass unnoticed unless they waited until nightfall. But in this terrain, travelling by night on bicycles would be exceedingly difficult and slow.

Bond decided to take the risk. He plotted a course that would keep them far away from the people he could see, taking advantage of dips in the terrain and keeping behind the cover of trees as much as possible. Maybe someone might see them from afar but why should two cyclists necessarily arouse suspicion? And in any event, even if that were to happen and they were reported, by the time the *Landwehr* geared into action, they would be long gone.

They crossed the first field diagonally, their bicycles' wheels constantly getting bogged down in the mud and their shoes sinking into it up to their ankles in some places.

The sun was high up and its rays warmed them. A far cry from yesterday's dampness and freezing cold.

After the field, a dirt road. They got back on their bicycles and followed the road to a grove of shade trees that provided shelter. The road dipped up ahead.

Bond dismounted, left his bicycle with Jenkins and went ahead on foot to survey the area. A few cows in the adjacent field gazed at him indifferently.

Ahead of him, more of the same: fields, scattered farmhouses, trees, a few people here and there further afield, a horse-drawn cart.

They continued on their way in the same manner until taking a midday break, once again, off the road in the woods. No one had bothered them, they hadn't spoken to anyone.

They shared a can of corned beef. They had to be careful about their consumption as they had no idea how and when they would be able to replenish their supplies.

Jenkins did not complain but he seemed tired. He struggled to his feet so that they could be on their way.

High in the cloudless sky, they saw hundreds of streaming trails, appearing like a shower of comets. They were the contrails from the engine exhaust of American bombers flying above, condensing in the cold temperatures at that altitude. They stopped and watched them in silence for a while. American bombers on their way back from a mission. They looked at each other, sharing the same thought: in 4 or 5 hours, those planes would be back on their bases in England, which to them now seemed so infinitely distant.

Later, on a paved road about one kilometre from where they were standing unseen behind a fence surrounding a field, they saw a military convoy, a motorcycle with its characteristic sidecar, a *Kübelwagen* and two Opel personnel carriers. The convoy continued on its way and was soon out of sight. There was no way of telling if it had anything to do with their escape, but it did serve to reaffirm Bond's decision to remain as much out of sight as possible.

In mid-afternoon they spotted up ahead some men working in a field. From the cover of a cluster of trees, Bond counted three men at work. The trail continued along one side of the field. If they followed it, they would certainly be seen. Otherwise they would have to circle around it, adding several kilometres to their journey, at least an hour's detour.

'What do you think?' Jenkins asked quietly.

'I don't think they're Germans,' Bond said. 'Look how they're dressed.'

The three men seemed to be gathering potatoes, shoving them into sacks then loading them onto a horse-drawn cart by the side of the road. They wore a patchwork of threadbare civilian and military clothing.

'They're POW's, Russian or Polish, slave labour,' Bond said, almost certain.

With the majority of the male population 18 to 50 years of age serving in the armed forces of the Reich, their places in the fields and factories were taken up by children, old people, women and foreign labourers, some of them voluntarily, like the Frenchmen Gary and Duvall, but most, like the millions of POW's[64] from the early years of the war, very much against their will, modern slaves from "inferior races", according to Nazi ideology.

'So what do we do?' Jenkins asked.

'Let's take a chance.'

'Okay.'

They came out of the woods, cycling at their normal pace and approached the field.

At some point, one of the men noticed them and spoke to the others. All three stood up and stared at Bond and Jenkins as they approached. They headed for their cart, one of them, mimicking the motions a smoker makes, crying out: 'Tabak, tabak!'

---

[64]   In 1941 alone, in the great encirclements of the central and southern Russian fronts during the Barbarossa campaign, the Germans took 1-1.5 million prisoners.

Bond stopped, shoved his hand into his pocket and pulling out a crumpled pack of cigarettes from the Red Cross parcels, gave it to him.

The man grabbed it eagerly, not believing his good fortune. He thanked Bond in broken German, pointing to himself and to the others, saying: 'Russki!'

Bond was about to move on when the Russian stopped him. He put a hand in one of the sacks on the cart, took out six large potatoes and offered them to Bond and Jenkins. They took them, expressed their thanks and rode off. When they were out of sight, Bond, to be on the safe side, changed course at the next intersection, heading south for a while before turning east again.

Dusk was approaching. They had to find shelter for the night. Barns and stables of inhabited farms were too dangerous. Many had dogs and even if they didn't, they would still be running the risk being discovered by some farmer.

A little before nightfall they got lucky. Bond spotted a half-ruined building, probably an abandoned warehouse, at the end of a dirt road that was overgrown with grass, suggesting it was no longer in use. They went in. Part of the roof had collapsed into a pile of broken beams and tiles, but most of it was intact, as were the walls.

'Aren't you afraid the Russians might turn us in?' Jenkins asked.

'Not likely. What would they say? That they ran into two cyclists? I'm sure they know nothing about the escape. Anyway, an interrogation by the Germans would only cause them grief.'

'What about the cigarettes?'

'They'll keep them for themselves. Anyway, they are available on the black market. Remember how popular they were with our camp guards?'

The floor was dirt but the part under the roof was dry. Bond and Jenkins gathered some firewood and even managed to pry loose a beam from the collapsed section of the roof. Bond soon had a fire going. At least tonight their clothes were dry other than being slightly damp from perspiration. He took one of the potatoes, opened a hole in it with J's knife and inserted a long twig, repeating the procedure with the rest of them. They propped them over the fire until they were cooked. Dinner consisted of corned beef and roast potatoes, topped off with a shot of schnapps.

Bond calculated that, as the crow flies, they must have covered at least another 25 kilometres. The lake had to be close by. But their food was running out, enough for just two more days at low rations.

And Jenkins' strength was showing signs of weakening, in spite of his determination and courage. Bond noted the sweat on his brow and frequent shortness of breath.

'How are you doing?' he asked.

'I'm okay…I think. Perhaps I caught a bit of a cold. It's nothing.'

They lay down on the ground to sleep. It was cold, an intrusive cold, not as intense as what they had felt in the forest of Sagan in the snow, but it soon penetrated their clothes, their socks and boots, and eventually deep down into their bodies. Bond got up and covered the sleeping professor with his other jacket.

In the morning, they shared a tin of milk and a tin of corned beef. Only two more tins of milk and four of corned beef remained.

'I miss the coffee, even ersatz,' Jenkins commented in an attempt at levity.

'Well, we do have a bit of English chocolate,' Bond replied, handing him a piece from the last of their supply. 'When we get back, I'll treat you to breakfast at the Savoy with all the coffee you can drink!'

'My treat as well, as my guest in Birmingham,' Jenkins replied.

They set off and soon could see the lake. At the first opportunity, they changed direction, turning south.

It was another sunny spring day, with just a few clouds occasionally hiding the sun. But Jenkins was lagging behind and Bond was forced to slow down the pace to allow him to keep up. A few times when Bond looked back at the professor, he saw him perspiring and wiping his brow. He could hear him coughing more and more frequently.

At one point, Bond saw an apple orchard behind a fence, with no one anywhere in sight. Leaving his bicycle with Jenkins, he scrambled over the fence, grabbed a few apples from the nearest tree and stuffed them in his pockets. He went back to Jenkins and handed him one as he bit into his own, peel and all.

Progress was agonisingly slow as they kept trying to avoid contact with people, detouring, seeking cover, avoiding villages and dwellings, Jenkins weakening more and more by the hour.

They stopped for a frugal lunch: corned beef, a little chocolate, an apple each. Bond studied his map again. As the crow flies, they had covered just ten kilometres all morning. And the toughest part of the journey lay ahead of them – the Bavarian Alps. With Jenkins in the state he was in, he wouldn't make it.

They had to find a safe place to hide out, to rest and to replenish their supplies…but where and how?

From the top of a hill, Bond surveyed the terrain again. In the distance he could see the Alps, still partly snow-covered, a major obstacle. Even he, in the good physical condition he was in, wouldn't be able to survive a night out there without shelter, let alone Jenkins. They would have to cross them in one go, in daylight. This meant they had to find a place to rest overnight at some point before they reached the mountains.

Around them, Bond took in the typical Bavarian landscape: fields, groves, villages and farmhouses, a sparsely inhabited area. Could they spend the night in a barn or stables? No other possible shelter was visible. It would be risky, but did they have any choice? A night out of doors could turn Jenkins' cold into pneumonia and that would be the end of it.

Which farm to choose? One that was especially isolated…he scrutinised the area more carefully.

It was late in the afternoon when Bond left Jenkins under the cover of some trees with the bicycles and proceeded cautiously on foot to his first choice, a farmhouse with a separate barn some 50 metres away from the house. Kneeling down behind the cover of a tree, he carefully studied the house and the barn, listening for any unwanted sounds. Open windows, certainly inhabited but, right now, not a soul in sight. The occupants were absent, probably not yet returned from the fields. They might make it into the barn at night…but he needed to explore the place better.

Bond broke his cover and started to approach the barn cautiously. He had hardly taken a few five steps when the silence was shattered by a dog's bark. Bond quickly went back to the cover of the tree and then hurried away, almost at a run, the sound of the barking slowly becoming weaker and weaker until he reached Jenkins some 300 metres back. Jenkins didn't have to ask how it had gone.

They took off again, heading to Bond's alternate choice. They lost their way a few times as paths crisscrossed, meandering through fields and woods, constantly changing direction with no clear pattern, until they finally found the place.

They had to pedal furiously across a 500-metre open stretch that separated two fields before making it to the protection of a small grove of trees surrounding the farm.

Bond left Jenkins with the bicycles on the edge of the woods at a spot where the ground dipped and some rocks and ferns formed a natural hiding place and continued on foot toward the farm. He came upon it in a clearing a short time later, the farmhouse on the one side and the barn a short distance away, separated by a dirt road.

Deserted and isolated.

Almost an ideal hideout, as long as there were no dogs around.

Doubled over, Bond headed for the nearest trees. He lay down behind one, remaining completely still for some time, trying to blend in with the surroundings.

He marshalled all his senses as he waited and watched.

All was quiet. No movement. A few birds twittered nearby. Further away, the rhythmic knock of a woodpecker seeking food, tapping away on a tree trunk with his beak. Insects buzzed around in front of his eyes. No barking, no sounds from the house or the barn.

Bond got up and approached the entrance of the barn as silently as he could.

Still no barking.

He reached the door, stood absolutely still. No sound, no movement.

Very gently, very carefully, he tried the door.

It wasn't locked and it opened with barely a sound. Thieves in this area, it seemed, were unknown. That, or there was nothing worth stealing. He peered into the darkened interior.

No movement, no sound.

His grip tightened on J's knife in his right hand. He pushed the door open further and went inside.

He was met by a loud noise, freezing him on the spot, until he realised it was just the sound of a cow mooing. The animal was in a stall to one side.

He smiled at the scare it had given him. It was even greater than anything he had encountered facing the enemy.

Aside from the cow, there was no sign of any other living creature in the large interior. To one side, stalls for animals, empty except for that single cow, on the other, further away from the door, bales of hay, probably the winter feed, various farm tools and machinery. The smell of straw, clover, manure, an earthy, but not unpleasant smell hit his nostrils. The air was cool, but considerably warmer than outside.

Bond left and returned to the professor.

'I think we've found shelter,' he told him, 'but better to wait until dark.' He wanted to make sure that they went in after the farm's owners had returned and put away any of their equipment before going in.

They sat in silence, waiting for nightfall. Bond waited for an additional hour to be on the safe side before starting out. Leaving their bicycles behind in the hideout, they walked through the dark woods, the distance to the farm seeming a lot longer than it had earlier, in the light of day.

They reached the edge of the woods and Bond looked around cautiously. The farmhouse and the barn were in darkness.

'Let's go,' he said.

They made their way to the barn, Bond opened the door, still unlocked, and they went in.

Aside from the cow, in the next stall there was now a horse as well, looking at them with its large eyes and a shake of its mane. So the farmers had returned and were probably already fast asleep. That was fine as far as Bond was concerned.

They moved to the back of the barn. They sat down on a bale of hay and ate their dinner: apple, corned beef, some schnapps, which was quickly running out, and some water from their canteens which Bond had filled at the pump over the water trough on their way over to the barn.

They made themselves comfortable as far away from the entrance as possible at the back of the barn, behind stacked bales of hay that hid them completely from any prying eyes that might possibly come near.

As he tried to get comfortable in the cramped space, Bond's hand inadvertently brushed against Jenkins' forehead. It was burning, but he was sleeping soundly, exhausted.

CHAPTER VI

Hiding

News of the escape reached C on Sunday.

He had no way of knowing who exactly had managed to escape, but since the breakout was from *Stalag Luft III* where Bond was being held, as confirmed by his card to his "aunt", C was sure, as sure as he could be under the circumstances, that Bond and Jenkins were among the escaped prisoners.

All he could do now was wait.

And hope.

He recalled Bond's escape plan as he had presented it to him before his departure.

There was not much he could do. But there was something…

He pressed the button on his intercom and said, 'Pritchett, I want to send out a coded message.'

• • •

Bond woke up, all senses alert, not on account of any noise but rather because his instincts had warned him to be on his guard.

He remained completely still, holding his breath, his knife gripped tightly in his fist.

Jenkins was asleep. As long as he didn't snore or make any noise in his sleep…

The door to the barn was opening. He couldn't see but he heard it creak, saw the interior brighten as the dawn forced its way inside through the doorway.

Bond and Jenkins were holed up in the darkest part of the barn. Bond was certain that they could only be seen if someone actually tripped over them…

He peered over the bales of hay and could distinguish a figure approaching the horse's stall. The person stopped and seemed to turn and stare in their direction. An illusion, Bond's nerves were on edge. There was no way they could have been heard or seen.

The person turned away from him again and took up the reins of the horse.

Suddenly the figure stopped again.

For a moment, Bond thought the person was going to look in their direction again but instead the person's gaze came to rest on a specific spot.

Bond followed the person's sightline.

Damn it!

Half-hidden next to a bale of hay, was Jenkins' knapsack that, after the fatigue and tension of the long day before, they had forgotten to make sure was hidden from sight.

The person walked over to the knapsack and letting go of the horse's reins, bent down over it, his back to Bond.

Bond sprang to his feet and, moving quickly, with his left arm he grabbed hold of the person around the neck, choking off any sound, ready to plunge the knife in his other hand into the heart.

At the last second, something held Bond back.

The person had frozen in fear.

Bond relaxed his grip around the neck slightly and whispered in German, 'If you cry out, you're dead. Are you alone?'

A strangled, 'Yes!' came in reply.

Bond relaxed his hold a little more and pulled back his knife, ready to use it again if necessary.

'Turn around,' he said. The person obeyed.

In the dim light he could just make out the face of a young woman, inches away from his own. He couldn't see the features clearly but it was without any doubt a girl.

'What's happening?' Jenkins asked, still half-asleep.

'We have a visitor,' Bond replied. "Everything's under control.' For the time being, he thought to himself.

'Is there anyone else in the house?' he asked the girl.

'No…I live alone,' she replied, struggling to hide the fear in her voice.

"Don't be afraid,' Bond said, his voice softening. 'Nothing will happen to you if you do as I say.'

He thought quickly.

The situation had altered radically.

He weighed the options. The first, leave immediately. He could immobilise the girl for hours, giving them time to get a good lead.

He never considered the option of killing the girl. He had never killed an unarmed civilian, and wasn't about to do so now, whatever the circumstances. But Jenkins' condition was such that the whole operation seemed doomed. There was no way he would be able to get through the snowbound Bavarian Alps on foot.

So then, what?

Perhaps fate was offering them an unexpected opportunity.

'Are you expecting anyone today?' he asked the girl.

She shook her head.

'Paul, find me some rope, a belt, anything,' Bond said.

Without asking why, Jenkins obeyed. He searched around the barn and came back with a length of rope.

'Don't be afraid,' Bond said again to the girl to reassure her. 'We're not criminals. Come.'

Keeping a hold on her, his knife at the ready, he led her to the animal stalls. 'Turn around,' he said.

He handed the knife to Jenkins and with a few quick movements tied the girl's hands behind her back to the upright beam of a stall. The girl, still frightened, didn't protest.

'Keep an eye on her,' he said to Jenkins. 'I'm going to take a look around the house.'

He poked his head out of the door and cautiously looked around. No one was there nor were there any sounds to be heard.

He approached the house, pausing to check again. Still nothing. He circled around the house, still on the alert.

Nothing.

He approached the entrance. He turned the door handle. It was unlocked and he pushed the door open. He went inside the house, bright with the light that was now streaming in through the unshuttered windows.

He found himself in the parlour, furnished simply in a rustic style, a wooden table with a white embroidered tablecloth, a few chairs around it, a sofa with two armchairs and another, a rocking chair, in front of the stone fireplace, photographs on the mantelpiece, what one would expect in any farmhouse, German or English. One door led to the kitchen, another to a narrow corridor with three doors, two bedrooms and a bathroom, all empty.

Bond confirmed that the girl had been telling the truth.

He returned to the stable.

He had made his decision.

The farmhouse was an ideal place to hide out and rest until Jenkins' cold passed and he was fit enough to travel.

He approached the girl.

'What's your name?' he asked.

'Sabine. Sabine Weber,' she replied.

'Sabine, we're going to have to stay here for a while,' he said. 'My friend here is not well. He has to rest. But we won't hurt you. I'm sorry for the inconvenience.' He smiled wryly at that comment.

He untied her hands, took the knife from Jenkins and still holding her, led her to the house, with Jenkins following closely behind. They went inside. Bond closed the door behind them, locking it. Only then did he finally release his hold on the girl.

'Do you have anything for us to eat?' he asked.

She nodded. 'In the kitchen.'

They followed her into the kitchen.

She opened a cupboard, took out bread, and from a small cooler, some cheese and milk.

'Should I warm the milk up?' she asked.

'Yes, and boil some water, as well,' he replied.

She obeyed, putting two small pots on the gas hobs of the small kitchen stove.

'Who are you?' she asked nervously.

'We're English airmen,' he answered. There was no longer any need to maintain their cover and pretend they were French engineers. Real French engineers would not be behaving like they were.

His reply didn't seem to upset her, on the contrary, she seemed relieved. Perhaps the fact they were Englishmen gave her a sense of security. After all, weren't English airmen, especially officers, gentlemen? And gentlemen were certainly not likely to hurt a young girl…

The milk was soon warm and the water boiled.

Bond took the two pots while Sabine took out two cups and two plates from a cupboard and brought them along with a few spoons to the table.

'For yourself as well,' Bond said to the girl.

The three of them sat at the table.

Bond rummaged through his knapsack and pulled out a couple of small treats that he had brought along for a special occasion: a packet of coffee and one of sugar, from the rest of their Red Cross supplies.

They hadn't used these up to now because they hadn't had a pot to boil water in.

He put coffee in the three cups and poured in the boiling water. The aroma flooded the room.

'Sugar?'

He put a little in each cup. Jenkins took a sip with obvious enjoyment. So did Sabine.

'I needed that,' Jenkins sighed. 'You really do think ahead, don't you? It never occurred to me to bring any along.'

'That's what they pay me for,' Bond joked.

The scene was unreal. Bond, Jenkins and Sabine, like three old friends, enjoying a bucolic breakfast somewhere in the south of Bavaria, as if they weren't enemies, as if there was no war going on.

Bond, as much as he had fought the Germans, did not see the girl as an enemy.

'Real coffee, real sugar,' Sabine broke the silence. 'It's been years since I had any. I had forgotten the taste.'

Bond looked at her closely.

Young, 20, 22. Blond hair, gathered up out of the way for work. Deep blue eyes, like a summer's sky, a Mediterranean sky. A slightly upturned nose, as if she were sniffing the air. A symmetrical oval face, a firm mouth, pearly white teeth visible between her lips. Her skin had the rosy freshness that working outdoors gives it in the early years, before longer-term exposure to the forces of nature furrows it like a tilled field. Free of makeup, without any lipstick, eye liner or powder, it was a lovely face.

She wore overalls, boots, a sturdy shirt and pullover for working outdoors. Bond could imagine a well-exercised, muscular body, a slim waist, hips widening just right.

Firm breasts, pushing out against her pullover as if straining to burst through. Bond realised he had touched them when his left arm reached around her neck to grab her earlier, his subconscious warning him not to use his knife.

Sabine sensed him observing her and in turn, examined him as discretely as she could, now that she felt somewhat calmer.

Grey-blue eyes, masculine features, black hair and stubble beginning to cover his cheeks and jaw (they had not shaved since Sunday morning in the hotel). A strong face, manly and attractive, that looked as if it were more suited to a Hollywood gangster movie, the private eye who never hesitated and was never afraid of anyone as he attempted to solve his case, no matter how mysterious and dangerous it was.

Sabine suddenly felt more at ease. No, she had nothing to fear from this man, as long as she did as she was told.

Nor from the other man, the older one, who looked neither like a gangster, nor a military man, but rather reminded her of a professor she had at school. She noticed the sweat on his brow, even though it was not hot in the room.

'Do you have a temperature?' she asked. Jenkins didn't understand the question in German.

'I'm afraid so,' Bond answered for him.

'I have a thermometer,' Sabine said. 'Shall I fetch it?'

She got up and Bond followed her to one of the two rooms at the back, her bedroom. She opened the drawer of the nightstand next to the bed, took out the thermometer and they returned to the parlour and gave it to Jenkins.

Upon removing it, Bond saw that the reading was 38.3 C.

'I have aspirin,' Sabine said, seeing Bond's expression.

'Where can he lie down?' he asked.

'In the other room. It's not being used.'

They led Jenkins to the room where he lay down. They returned to the parlour.

'I have to milk the cow,' Sabine said.

They left the house, Bond ready to stop her if she tried to run. The girl headed to the barn. Bond followed her and closed the door behind them after they went in, just to be on the safe side.

Sabine picked up a bucket that was in the corner, went over to the cow's stall, sat on a stool and began to milk the animal while Bond stood watching her. When she finished, she gave the cow a bunch of clover and then did the same for the horse.

They left the stable. Bond impulsively took the bucket of milk from her hand and carried it to the house.

What would C think if he could see him now, carrying a bucket of milk for a young German girl on an isolated Bavarian farm? Probably think he had lost his mind. Though, maybe not. Many times C grasped things that others could not. Must be one of the necessary virtues of a successful leader.

They went into the house and Bond locked the door behind him. When she had put away the milk, Sabine said, 'I have to cook.'

In the kitchen, Bond sat down always keeping an eye on her. Sabine took a cabbage, chopped it up, put a pot of water to boil and tossed the cabbage in. Bond kept a close watch on the knife. If she tried anything, he knew that he wouldn't have any trouble disarming her, what with his SAS training. But the girl didn't make the slightest move. In a second pot, she put a few potatoes on to boil.

They returned to the parlour.

'Can I do some knitting?' she asked.

He nodded.

Sabine took up her knitting needles and yarn from the small table in front of the sofa and began to knit.

Bond remained standing beside the fireplace, discretely observing her, as her hands skilfully worked the knitting needles. How did she fill those hours of solitude after the work on the farm was done, or in the winter when she couldn't work outdoors?

He glanced at the photographs on the mantelpiece. An elderly couple, probably her parents. A lieutenant commander in the *Kriegsmarine* with a medal, a tiny metal submarine, the sign of the *Ubootswaffe*[65], pinned to his chest, smiling into the camera. A young man, in the black uniform of the *Panzerwaffe*[66], also with a carefree smile, his tank visible in the background.

---

[65] *Kriegsmarine*: The German Navy. *Unterseebootswaffe*: The submarine service. May 1943 marked the peak of the Battle of the Atlantic. Losses in submarines from Allied aircraft and escort ships were so great that month that their commander, Admiral Dönitz, was obliged to call off missions in the Atlantic.

[66] *Panzer*: armour, a tank. In July 1943, the Germans conducted their last great assault on the Eastern Front, in an attempt to encircle Kursk. In the midst of this, the assault led to the biggest battle involving armoured vehicles in history, around the village of Prohorovka. Heavy losses and the Allied landings in Sicily forced Hitler to call off the assault.

Sabine looked up, noticing him looking at the photographs.

'Your parents?' Bond asked.

She nodded.

'Where are they?'

'They've passed away,' she replied.

And, anticipating Bond's next question, or perhaps simply feeling the need to unburden her soul, she went on:

'The naval officer is Werner, my fiancé. He never came back from a mission in May of last year. The other is Peter, my brother, killed at Kursk in July. My father died of a heart attack in 1941. My mother lived with me. She died in November. I think she couldn't stand so much death…'

Bond said nothing. An "I'm sorry" would sound hollow, hypocritical. But her words did explain why she lived alone.

He looked around. A poor household, but pleasant, the few pieces well-laid out, everything spotless, two paintings of landscapes on the walls, a few vases, two brass candlesticks, a carpet, the white embroidered curtains on the windows, embroidered tablecloth, probably her own work.

On one wall, a library. Bond went over to take a closer look. A few classic German novels: Mann, Hesse, Goethe, Lessing and others, more recent. The presence of Hesse and Mann came as a surprise, they were not favourites of the Nazis and both had left Germany. On a lower shelf, books on architecture.

Sabine was watching him and again anticipated his next question.

'When I was in high school, I wanted to become an architect. Before the war. In the days when we felt an unprecedented enthusiasm, a time when everything seemed possible. When we were proud to be German. We believed in the future. We dreamed, we saw our dreams become reality. A new Germany, released from the defeat in war, free from inflation, unemployment and unrest was being born, expressing itself in new projects going up everywhere, highways, public buildings, stadiums, the sites for the Olympic Games of 1936...'

Sabine fell silent, as if she was unable to continue.

'You didn't continue your studies? Why?'

'By the time I finished school, the war had begun. It was no time for studying. My brother had joined the army. My father died. We had to survive. Then finally, there was only myself and the farm...'

'The war will end,' Bond said. 'Soon. You can continue your studies then. You're very young.'

'You think so? In a Germany in ruins, crushed?'

'All the more reason. Germany will need architects to rebuild once again.'

Sabine did not answer. She put aside her knitting needles, rose and went into the kitchen to check on the food. She added a large piece of pork to the cabbage.

They sat down for lunch. Sabine set the table with a clean tablecloth and napkins, cutlery, glasses and a bottle of German wine from the Rhine region.

The food was simple, but filling and delicious. Bond felt his strength returning and so did Jenkins. Sabine prepared a cup of herbal tea for him and he went back to bed.

Sabine picked up her knitting again.

'May I take a book?' Bond asked.

She nodded.

He took down Hesse's *Steppenwolf* and sat down to read.

The afternoon passed. Quietly and peacefully, the way it would have been with any rural family anywhere in Europe if a war hadn't been raging.

When it started to get dark, Sabine said:

'We'll need wood for the fireplace. And some for the stove in the room where your friend is resting.'

They went together to the barn and came back with logs. Bond stacked some in the fireplace and lit a fire. Then they went to Jenkins' room and stoked the stove there.

For dinner, Sabine prepared a very filling omelette with cheese and bacon together with bread. 'I knead and bake it myself,' she told them.

Though early, it was time to go to bed. Here, time followed the pattern of day and night, as it always did in the countryside: sleeping shortly after dusk and waking up just before dawn – not like it did in the city.

Bond allowed Sabine the use of the bathroom after making sure the window was too small for her to squeeze through. He kept a discrete eye on the half-open door. When she came out, he followed her to her bedroom. He turned his back to allow her to change into a woollen nightgown. He allowed her to lie down and then he went up to her.

'What are you doing?' she asked, suddenly alarmed again.

'Don't be afraid. Just a precaution for the night.'

He gently pulled her arms over her head and tied them to the headboard with rope he had taken from the stable, making sure she couldn't reach the knots. He tied down her feet as well.

'It might be a little uncomfortable, but I hope you can get to sleep. Good night.'

Sabine didn't reply.

Bond went back to the parlour, lay down on the sofa and covered himself with a blanket she had given him. The fire glowed faintly, warming the room pleasantly. He fell into a peaceful sleep to the gentle crackling of the fire. The sofa was definitely more comfortable than the variety of floors they had slept on the last few nights - the cabin, the ruin and the barn.

He woke up feeling refreshed and in good spirits. He was first in the bathroom, he shaved and washed up. Then he went to Sabine's room. She was awake and watched him with her big eyes, as if she wanted to tell him something. He untied her with a cheerful, 'Good morning.'

'I hope you managed to get some sleep,' he added.

A short time later, they sat down to a breakfast of warm milk, bread and cheese. Jenkins' temperature had dropped and he was already feeling better.

'Can we go out to the fields?' Sabine asked. 'There are jobs that I must tend to.'

Bond and the woman hitched the horse to the wagon and soon reached the field on the other side of the woods, about a kilometre from the farmhouse, quite isolated. Bond surveyed the terrain. The field was flanked by woods on one side and a cluster of trees opposite. The other two sides were open, offering a clear view of the areas beyond. In the distance, he could make out tiny figures of people at work. He remained on the edge of the field under cover of the trees keeping an eye on the girl and the people in the other fields. No one came near.

The girl, kneeling on the ground, dug up potatoes, putting them in a sack. After filling two sacks she said that it was enough for the day. Bond picked them up and loaded them onto the cart.

They returned to the barn where Sabine fed and watered the horse and milked the cow, then fed her as well.

Back at the house, Bond lit the fire, while she put two large pots of water to boil on the stove. She prepared a pan with sliced potatoes and a few pieces of pork, putting it in the oven to roast.

When the water had boiled, she carried the two pots into the bathroom. Bond realised that the house didn't have a water boiler.

A while later, Sabine emerged from the bathroom. She had changed into fresh clothes and her hair was loose, bronze tresses with golden highlights cascading almost down to her waist.

They sat down to eat, at first in silence. The food was rather dull, but tasty and filling, immeasurably better than the corned beef they had been subsisting on during the last few days.

'Don't you have any friends? Acquaintances? Relatives?' Bond asked.

'I have a married aunt in Regensburg and a married uncle in Munich,' she replied.

'You haven't considered moving in with either of them?'

'They have families, children…I don't want to be a burden. Anyway, life in the cities is more difficult now. Food is rationed, there are the bombings…Here at least I'm almost self-sufficient. I barter with any excess produce, potatoes, milk, vegetables, once a week in the village, for whatever I lack.'

'Friends, boyfriends? Don't you ever go to the village in the evenings?'

She didn't answer right away. Then, as if she had arrived at a difficult decision, she started to speak:

'A man named Hans Finger lived on one of the nearby farms. He was around 65. He had a daughter, married, living in Schweinfurt, a son killed in action in Africa in 1942 and another on the Eastern Front. His wife had died. Herr Finger worked his farm on his own as the government urged us all to do. Everyone, the young, the old, the women, had to work for the good of the Reich, for the war effort, farming, breeding livestock, in the factories, since most of the men were in the armed forces.

'Herr Finger asked to be given a helper, which was not unusual. He was sent a

Polish girl, Zofia, around my age. A willing and hard-working girl who I would sometimes run into in the village. Whenever we happened to be working in the fields at the same time, we would help one another. She didn't speak German very well but we still became friends. Same age, same jobs, both lonely…On some afternoons, after work, or when the weather was not good for working outdoors she would come over here or I would go to Herr Finger's. We would sit and knit, or cook. She frequently sat where you're sitting now…'

She paused as if something had caught in her throat. After a while, she continued, determined to tell her story.

'Herr Finger was a good man. He didn't treat her like a slave, which was what she was, in effect, like all the prisoners that are brought here to work in the fields. He treated her well. But one day the inevitable happened. They had an affair. This sort of thing was quite common and was usually either ignored by the authorities, or they turned a blind eye, even though it was forbidden under the race laws.[67] Everything would have been fine if it hadn't been for a man named Schultz.

'Schultz is the party leader in the village. Around 45, he's always boasting that he had participated in the Beerhall Putsch in Munich and that he personally knows the *Führer*. Because of his position, he's been able to avoid serving in the armed forces. He's a man who loves to boast, to be feared. He drinks a lot and when he does, he becomes very belligerent and vulgar. He thinks his position allows him to do anything he wants. He's a pig!

'He used to chase after me but as long as Werner was alive, he was cautious about it. After Werner was killed, that changed and he began making suggestive comments, groping, always trying to touch me every chance he got, supposedly by accident. So I kept my visits to the village at a minimum.

'Schultz had a history with Finger. Finger was a Social Democrat and had never joined the Nazi Party like most people did in 1933. Neither did he bow down to Schultz like everyone else did.

'I don't know how Schultz found out about or suspected Finger's affair with Zofia. But he denounced them, they were tried and convicted. Schultz was the main witness against them and had his cronies back him up.'

---

[67]   *Rassengesetz:* Race laws in Nazi Germany forbade any mixing of Aryan Germans with "inferior races" such as the Slavs.

Sabine paused again, overcome with emotion, struggling to continue:

'Zofia was executed. Finger was sentenced to ten years in prison, only because he was German and his sons were in the armed forces...'

Bond didn't interrupt her. Jenkins, though not understanding anything, sensed her distress and said nothing, waiting for Bond to explain later.

'For a few days I didn't feel like facing anyone, certainly no one from the village and especially not Schultz or any of his cronies. But I couldn't accept it. I was boiling inside, my anger festering, clouding my judgement, drowning any other feelings. Until one night I just couldn't take it anymore. I went to the *Bierstube* in the village where every night Schultz sat drinking with his cronies. I found him, tankard of beer in hand, drinking and speaking loudly as he always did when he was in a jolly mood.

'"Sabine, come have a drink with us," he said, inviting me to join him.

'I went over to him without saying anything. When I reached him, I slapped him hard. His raised tankard shook and his beer spilled all over him. Then I turned around and walked right out, leaving everyone there stunned, speechless.'

Sabine fell silent.

'That was a very brave thing to do,' Bond commented.

'Brave? At that moment I wasn't giving any thought to the consequences. I was doing it for Zofia. And for myself.'

'And after that?'

'Schultz is a coward. He didn't do anything, even though he had been made a fool of. I was a dead war hero's fiancée and the sister of another. Perhaps he was afraid I would accuse him of harassment. In any event, he did nothing. Since then I only go to the village if it's absolutely necessary, and never at night. The villagers avoid me because they are afraid of Schultz, though I think many of them secretly approve of what I did.'

They finished their meal in silence. Jenkins retired with an herbal tea and some aspirin. Sabine prepared for bedtime. When she laid down Bond tied her up as he had done the night before. She looked at him with an expression Bond couldn't fathom.

He bent down and kissed her lightly on the lips.

She was startled but didn't appear upset.

Sabine remained awake for some time. Telling her story at last had made her feel that a weight had been lifted from her soul. Relating it to a stranger, an invader, an enemy, to this rugged young man...in whom she felt an inexplicable trust, perhaps because he was a stranger had made it easier. His kiss had made her shiver. He had her in his absolute power and this frightened her a little – but also excited her at the same time.

Now that he was alone, Bond put two large pots of water to boil as Sabine had done the previous night and had his first hot bath since Saturday.

He slept refreshed on the sofa.

The next morning Jenkins no longer had any temperature and he was in good spirits, feeling much stronger.

'I think it's time we move on,' he said to Bond. 'You've been taking care of me like a baby long enough.'

Bond announced to Sabine that they were going to leave the next morning. He accompanied her to the fields once again where she took her cow to graze on the first shoots of grass that had appeared after the snows had melted. It was cloudy but the temperature had gone up. That evening, Sabine prepared knudel with cream and cheese.

'Tomorrow it's Saturday and I'm taking the cart to market to sell my produce and buy what I need. I can take you up to there. It will be less tiring for you,' Sabine suggested over dinner.

Bond discussed this with Jenkins and they agreed to accept the offer. The bicycles would be more of a burden than a help on the mountain roads they had to tackle. They decided to leave them behind. With the cart and on foot, their chances would be better.

So the next morning after Sabine and Bond had led the cow out to pasture and after a good breakfast, they prepared for their departure. They hitched the horse to the cart, loaded the sacks of potatoes and the milk cans, and shouldered their knapsacks, lighter now, but full of bread and cheese, an offering from Sabine. They started off, Jenkins in the cart with the sacks, Bond sitting next to her.

It was the first day of April, a sunny, beautiful spring day.

• • •

Benno sat gazing at his map of the Reich as he had been doing frequently during the past several days. It helped him think.

Most of the escaped POW's had been apprehended. Still at large were two Norwegians, a Dutchman and two Britishers. And one of them was Rodger.

They had vanished as if they had been swallowed up by the earth. Was it possible that they had already reached neutral territory, having evaded all the blockades and checkpoints? One couldn't ignore that possibility...

But then again, perhaps they were still in the Reich, waiting for the hue and cry of the manhunt to die down, for our vigilance to wane, in hiding somewhere. Just like when we were hunting down Heydrich's murderers in Prague, he mused.[68]

Benno was a persistent and patient man, like any good policeman... like any good officer. He remembered his uncle's words: "Benno, a good hunter must learn to be patient and to persevere. So must a good pilot. The pilot that seeks out encounters at any opportunity under any conditions may quickly win many victories, but eventually he will wind up a dead hero, just like Werner Voss.[69] The good pilot who manages to survive is the one who is patient, attacking only when he has the advantage."

Benno kept that notion in mind. The two Britishers (he suspected they were travelling together), like hunted prey, must have found a good place to hide out. But at some point, they would have to abandon it and emerge.

Up to now, the police, the *Landwehr* and the *Hitlerjugend* had done their job well and had apprehended most of the escaped

---

68   Reinhard Heydrich, Acting Reich Protector of Bohemia and Moravia, what had been Czechoslovakia before the war, and one of the highest officers in the Nazi hierarchy. In 1942, Czech resistance fighters assassinated him with a bomb planted under his car. They hid in a crypt in a church but were discovered, perhaps betrayed, and died in a gun battle with the Germans.

69   Voss was a German ace of WWI with 48 victories. Flying one of the first of the new Fokker tri-planes, on his own, he attacked a British formation of five Sopwith Camels. He was killed in that epic battle.

prisoners. But perhaps now was the time to employ other methods. Like SS patrols at the borders. At all the borders, the last net in which to snare the fugitives if they were still within the Reich.

Benno decided to contact Schellenberg, to explain the situation and request his approval.

CHAPTER VII

Dying

Sabine left her cow out in the pasture to graze. Then she hitched the horse to the cart and with Bond's help loaded the sacks and barrels of produce for sale on board. She locked the front door of the farmhouse and they set off.

They came out onto the dirt road that led to the village. A little while later they turned off onto a wider road that led south, winding uphill into the Bavarian Alps. The mountain slopes were heavily forested for the most part and the peaks were still snow-covered at this time of year.

The horse ambled on at a normal pace. Bond and Sabine were silent, each absorbed in their own thoughts. They encountered the usual traffic, farmers going to or from the village, either on foot or by horse-drawn cart. Bond estimated that the village lay along the old German-Austrian border. Since the *Anschluß*[70] there was no longer

---

[70]   *Anschluß:* The annexation of Austria to the Reich by Hitler in 1938.

any border as Austria was now part of the Reich. And accordingly, no border controls either.

'I can take you further,' Sabine said suddenly, as if she had been thinking about it for some time but had just come to a decision. 'I'll drop you off before we reach the village. There's a narrow dirt road that skirts around it. It's rarely used and barely visible from the village. I'll tend to my affairs and then I'll come and pick you up…'

'Why would you do this?' Bond asked.

Sabine shrugged. 'I don't know,' she admitted. 'Perhaps because I can't stand this life any longer…Perhaps for Zofia…You never told me your name,' she added, changing the subject.

'Andrew,' he said.

'Well then, Andrew?'

He thought for a while. Certainly the more distance they covered on the cart the better…but how far could he trust her?

As if reading his thoughts, she asked, 'Don't you trust me?'

'You're doing something very dangerous…that's not necessary,' he replied.

'Must we always do only what's necessary?' she asked with intensity. 'Can't we ever do simply what our hearts tell us to?'

And as if having said more than she had intended, she added, 'It's Saturday, there's nothing waiting for me back home…'

Bond decided to accept the offer. Taking a risk but, then again, up to now, that's all they had been doing. He had learned to let logic guide him, but whenever logic couldn't provide an answer, then he followed his heart.

'Very well. Where will you pick us up afterward?'

At a bend in the road, out of sight of the village, Sabine stopped for them to get off. She showed them where the detour began on the other side of the road, half-hidden by the trees, and explained where they would meet.

Their knapsacks on their backs, Bond and Jenkins started off at a brisk pace. They bypassed the village and reconnected with the road beyond its southern edge, higher up the hill. Bond found the spot that Sabine had described, an old stone roadside shrine. He looked around. The road wound upwards between the forested and still snowbound hills. The sunlight sparkled on the snow.

'Let's climb up there,' Bond pointed to a spot under the trees above the road where they could keep a lookout unobserved. If they saw anything suspicious then they could always melt back into the forest.

They waited there for about half an hour, observing the road and the village further down. All they saw were two carts that looked empty, farmers returning to their farms.

Bond finally spotted Sabine's cart leaving the village, approaching at a slow pace so as not to draw any attention. He confirmed that no one was following her.

Next to him Jenkins whispered, 'What deal have you made with lady luck?'

'What do you mean?' Bond asked without taking his eyes off the cart.

'Of all the farms in Bavaria, to be led to Sabine's!' Jenkins said.

'Always trust in lady luck!' Bond said with a smile. 'Let's go!!'

The cart had come to a stop next to the shrine.

They climbed down from their hideout and got on board, taking the same places they had earlier.

They set off again up the climbing, winding road into the Tyrolean countryside so familiar to Bond. It seemed to have been forgotten by the war, the only exception, the absence of the foreign visitors who usually swarmed over this region in peacetime. Mountains all around, not especially steep nor jagged, forming valleys and pastures where black and white and brown cows grazed wherever the snow had melted, isolated farm houses, chalets, forests of fir trees, a peaceful and bucolic landscape.

It was past three when the horse began to show signs of exhaustion because of the continuous uphill climb. Sabine stopped.

'I don't think she can take any more,' she said.

They all stepped down. It was time to part company.

'Sabine, I don't know what to say,' Bond said, meaning it sincerely. Words were inadequate.

'Will you accept something from us?' he asked, preparing to give her three of the gold sovereigns.

She looked at him with her innocent deep blue eyes that reflected the colour of the sky and the radiance of the sun.

'I'm coming with you,' she said simply.

Bond's hands stopped in mid-air. He couldn't believe what he had just heard.

'I'm coming with you. To Switzerland. Isn't that where you're going? I have nothing to keep me here,' she added.

Jenkins had grasped what she was saying, hearing the word "*komme*".

Bond shook his head, still unable to believe what she had said. He finally exclaimed, 'Have you really thought this out?'

'I've been thinking about this for months, now. I feel as if I'm choking to death here...but alone, I never had enough courage to do it. Now I've made my decision. I'm going, either with you or alone, following behind you. But I'm not going back!'

Bond didn't know how to deal with this startling development. How would her presence affect his plan, especially now that they were so close to their destination? Would it be to their advantage or a hindrance? He was trained to deal with the unexpected - but this?

Jenkins made the decision for both of them.

'Let her come,' he said.

Sabine understood. She went up to her horse and caressed his forehead. Unhitching him, she led him away from the cart to the side of the road. She took an apple out of the bag on her shoulder and fed it to the horse. Looking at her with his gentle eyes, the horse started to chew on the apple.

'What will happen to him?' Bond asked.

'Someone will find him and take him. Horses are very much in demand by the villagers...so many of them have been requisitioned by the army. Let's go,' she said, her voice choking a little from emotion as she gave the horse one last caress on the forehead.

'We're going to Kitzbühel, aren't we?' Sabine guessed.

Bond nodded.

She continued, 'I know a less travelled road.' She shouldered her knapsack and started walking without even a glance behind her, as if turning her back on her old life.

They followed her at a rapid pace. It was dusk when they caught their first glimpse of the town.

Familiar, just as Bond remembered it from his many vacations there. The main street with its three- and four-storey houses and peaked roofs, some still snow-covered, others with stalactites hanging from their eaves, releasing large drops of water that fell onto the pavement. The houses were stuck together, one next to the other, like a herd of animals huddling together for warmth. Some of the trees lining the street were already showing signs of their first spring leaves. He could make out the two creeks that encircled the old centre of the town and its two churches, the *Pfarrkirche* and the *Liebfrauenkirche,* next to each other, the latter with its tall square bell tower that ended in an odd, bulbous cone that seemed as if it was trying to pierce through the heavens.

The narrow valley was shut off at the far end by the rising peaks of the Alps of Kitzbühel, where Bond in the past had spent so many carefree days learning to ski.

Bond found his bearings by bringing to mind familiar landmarks to guide him to his destination. This was another reason he had chosen their unusual route for the escape.

They waited in the woods for night to fall before entering the town. This time, Bond took the lead. At first, he had a little difficulty in the dark finding the landmarks he was looking for. He was used to the town full of the bright lights and boisterous crowds of peacetime vacationers, not darkened by the blackout, silent, almost as if uninhabited. After following the main street into town for a while, Bond recognized the intersection he was looking for and they turned off the main street onto an alley that eventually led them up to a darkened, isolated chalet on the outskirts.

Bond reconnoitred the area. Were the occupants he knew still there? Perhaps things had changed. One more necessary risk he had decided to take.

From one of the shuttered window a very faint light glowed, a sign that the chalet was occupied.

'Wait here,' he whispered to the others, leaving them behind in the dark.

He climbed the three steps to the chalet's entrance, listened carefully, threw a cautionary glance into the darkness around him to confirm that there was no one about and that Sabine and Jenkins were out of sight. He raised his hand and after a brief pause, he rang the doorbell.

He heard the bell ring in the house, the sound muffled.

He stood back, waiting, alert.

Nothing.

He rang again, almost feeling, counting his every heartbeat.

Finally, a sound from inside. A voice that he would recognise anywhere.

'Ja, ja, ich komm!' He heard the key turning in the lock. The door opened a crack, spilling light outside.

Bond stepped into the light so he could be seen.

The man stood there, his hand frozen in the air, speechless, paralysed, as if he had seen a ghost. In fact, Bond's presence was just as startling as if he had really been a ghost.

'It's me, Herr Sonderhauser,' Bond assured him.

'Andrew, you?' the other man stammered, still finding it difficult to believe his eyes.

'It's me,' Bond repeated. 'Can I come in?'

'But of course, of course! Come in!' His voice warmed in welcome.

'I have two friends with me,' Bond said and without pausing for a response he turned and whispered loudly so he could be heard by the others: 'Come on over!'

Sabine and Jenkins quickly emerged from the darkness and they all stepped into the chalet. Sonderhauser closed and locked the door behind them.

'Please, sit down,' he said.

'This is Paul and Sabine,' Bond said, introducing his companions. 'Herr Sonderhauser. He taught me how to ski before the war…he was like a father to me, at a time when I really needed one,' he added, as if he felt a need to justify himself.

Suddenly, a woman's voice was heard:

'Who is it?' A woman wrapped in a robe entered the parlour. She saw the three visitors, immediately recognizing the one - much thinner, with a trace of a beard, more mature, but with that same expression that had always spoken such volumes to her, now a man, no longer the boy whom she had regarded somewhat as an adopted son.

'Andrew!' she cried, rushing to him and embracing him warmly. 'Andrew!' she repeated, unable to believe that he was actually there. 'It's been so long…'

'Five years,' Bond murmured. 'Since August of '39. But it feels as if only days have passed since then.'

'Have you eaten?' Frau Sonderhauser asked, suddenly remembering her duties as the hostess. Without waiting for a reply, she went on, 'I'll put something together right away. Wilhelm, won't you offer our guests a drink?'

He got up, fetched four glasses, a bottle of liqueur and another of schnapps.

'I'm sorry I can't offer you a Martini, Andrew,' he apologised with a twinkle in his eye. 'The shortages of war, you know…'

'No need. Frau Sonderhauser's liqueur is far better than anything else,' Bond replied.

Tantalising aromas wafted from the kitchen. Bond didn't want to relate the story of how they had ended up here until Frau Sonderhauser could hear it as well. They engaged in small talk until they were called to the table.

The dinner consisted of sausages and fried potatoes, accompanied by a local Tyrolean white wine, and followed by baked apples with syrup, topped with great dollops of real whipped cream. The cows in this region obviously continued to produce excellent milk despite the war.

Over dinner, Bond related how they had come to Kitzbühel, omitting only the true identity of Jenkins. It was a necessary precaution, not only for themselves but for the Sonderhausers as well.

'Unbelievable!' Sonderhauser exclaimed. 'This damned war!'

'Can we stay the night? Or are we endangering you too much?' Bond asked.

'Nonsense, Andrew! Danger? As if nothing is dangerous in this life of ours with those crazy people running our country and destroying Germany!' Sonderhauser burst out. 'Of course you can stay. As long as you have to. Our house is isolated and we're not expecting any visitors.'

'It won't be for too long,' Bond said, relieved. His intuition had proved to be correct: Sonderhauser was still the same man he had known before the war.

'And after? What will you do?'

'Do you still have your *Käfer*[71]? Bond asked. 'May we borrow it? If there's a problem you can claim it was stolen…'

Sonderhauser waved away Bond's suggestion.

'Nonsense, Bond. Of course I still have it and I would gladly give it to you…the trouble is, there is no fuel available for private citizens. All of it is reserved for the war effort. I don't think there's enough petrol in the tank for even 20 kilometres.'

'How about on the black market?' Bond asked. 'I hear that anything can be had…'

'That's true but for a price - and on one wants to accept *Reichsmarks*…'

'That's not a problem,' Bond said with a smile, taking three gold sovereigns from his pocket and placing them on the table.

'Then that problem is indeed solved…I'll be off in the morning… I'll arrange everything,' Sonderhauser said. 'One more thing, Andrew,' he added, upon reflection. 'I'll drive you myself wherever you want to go…'

'I can't ask that of you, Herr Sonderhauser. It's too great a risk…'

---

[71]   *Käfer*: German for "Beetle", the Volkswagen model that first circulated in 1939

'Nonsense, Andrew! These last several years I've done a few things I'm not very proud of. It's time to do something right.' He hesitated momentarily and then continued, as if he needed to get something off his chest.

'I joined the Party, Andrew, you know that…and I voted for Hitler in 1933. You and I had argued about that at the time. But I believed in his ideas about a strong Germany, proud, united, reborn. What an idiot I was! How he fooled us! How did we end up this way? What will become of us, Andrew?'

'The war won't last much longer,' Bond responded softly. You're not the only ones he fooled, after all. What about the French, the British, the Russians…even Mr. Chamberlain…?'

'Yes, but we are the ones who brought him to power. I didn't know, Andrew, I just never could have imagined!'

'Stop your whining,' Frau Sonderhauser broke in sternly. 'Our guests are tired. They must rest.'

She rose from the table and escorted Sabine and Jenkins to their rooms. The chalet was large and in the good old days they used to rent out a few rooms to tourists. Bond lingered behind with Sonderhauser.

'What are your plans, Andrew?'

Bond laid out his two alternatives. The one plan was to cross the Alps here at Kitzbühel through the Thurn Pass, come out in the Tal Valley and cross into the Italian Tyrol where he would join up with Italian anti-Fascist partisans he knew were active in that area. Not a very promising plan. It would be a difficult run through snow-covered mountains, only to end up in yet another Axis country.

The second alternative depended on the availability of fuel.

'Don't worry, I'll find some,' Sonderhauser assured him. 'I know the people who handle the fuel supplies for the *Landwehr*. You can't imagine how easy it is to make fuel mysteriously disappear!'

They sat a while longer, talking about the pre-war days until Bond rose to retire. He insisted upon not overstaying their welcome despite Sonderhauser's offer for them to stay as long as they wanted. Every delay, for whatever reason, was dangerous for all concerned.

They woke up early and Frau Sonderhauser prepared them a filling breakfast of milk, bread, butter and her own homemade jam. Her husband had gone out but he returned as they were finishing their meal, with good news:

'Everything has been taken care of! My friend at the *Landwehr* warehouse seemed very moved when I told him I needed the petrol to visit my elderly aunt who is ill, in Innsbruck.'

'Do you actually have an aunt in Innsbruck?' Sabine asked.

'I do, but she's not ill and I'm sure she'll outlive us all,' Sonderhauser said with a laugh. 'But, just in case, I will visit her on my way back!'

Sonderhauser loaded some things into the boot of the automobile, a 1939 Beetle. Frau Sonderhauser hugged Bond tightly, visibly moved. 'You be careful, Andrew!'

'I will! And I'll be back to visit you when the war is over!'

Sabine sat in front next to Sonderhauser with Bond and Jenkins in the back.

They set off, driving through Kitzbühel. Leaving town, they spied two policemen. Sonderhauser came to a stop and rolled down his window.

'Good morning, Herr Zaretski!' he said, recognising the one.

Kitzbühel was a small town and Sonderhauser, as a member of the *Landwehr,* had frequent contact with the police.

'Good morning to you, too, Herr Sonderhauser. Early today, I see. You have company,' he commented in a friendly fashion.

'Old customers and friends,' Sonderhauser responded casually. 'They've come to visit and relive old memories.'

'And it's such a perfect day!' the policeman observed.

As indeed it was. A bright, sunny spring Sunday with the snow on the mountain slopes glistening, a blue sky marred only by two small, white clouds.

'What are you here for?' Sonderhauser asked innocently.

'We had a message a few days ago to be on the lookout for some escaped British prisoners…you received the same message at the *Landwehr.* As if from all the places in the Reich they would chose Kitzbühel for a vacation!!' Zaretski laughed at his own joke and Sonderhauser joined in.

Zaretski knew Sonderhauser not only as a member of the *Landwehr* but also as a Party member. Of course, in recent months he hadn't been very active, but the same was true of himself and many others who were keeping up appearances, but with a heavy heart. The closer the Allies advanced on the borders of the Reich, the more the zeal of many members was waning. In any event, they were Austrians and Hitler had annexed their country to the Reich by force. From one point of view, they too were victims. He preferred to forget the enthusiasm with which he had greeted the *Anschluß* back then.

The policeman waved them on and they started off again. They got onto the main road to Innsbruck, encountering very little traffic on the way, a small military convoy, two or three private cars, a few horse-drawn carts and some cyclists as they neared the city. They drove right on through, leaving the city from the east, heading for Arlberg, following the route alongside the Inn River.

Just as they were leaving the city, they were stopped by policemen again.

Sonderhauser handed over his papers. He included his Party membership identification. The officer in charge glanced at them briefly, noting the Party membership. He examined Sabine's papers as well and returned them to her. He took a little longer studying the papers of the two foreigners.

'Where are you going?' he asked rather indifferently.

Sonderhauser offered his most disarming smile. 'Visiting my aunt. Monsieur Gary is and old customer and friend. He's come to visit his fiancée…an opportunity for a Sunday excursion for us all.'

The policeman returned their papers and as a typical polite Austrian wished them a pleasant journey. Not the slightest suspicion crossed his mind. Who could ever imagine, British fugitives travelling at high noon on the main road out of Innsbruck in the company of a German woman and driven by a member of the Party, in the *Landwehr* no less!

Leaving Innsbruck, Sonderhauser took the road to Arlberg that ran along the Inn River valley between the Bavarian Alps to the north and the Lotztal Alps to the south, toward the once multi-ethnic region of the Finstermunz, the point where Switzerland meets with Italy and Austria. He was especially cautious, frequently stopping the VW to walk on ahead and survey the road before them to check for roadblocks or patrols. He didn't want to take any chances now that they were so close to their objective.

But there were no roadblocks, no patrols. It seemed as if the authorities had chosen to rely only on the guard posts outside of Innsbruck and naturally, at the border itself.

They drove through villages and towns encountering the usual light Sunday traffic but not a single obstacle. Anyway, what was so odd about an automobile with number plates from Kitzbühel? They passed through Imst, Zams, Landeck with its ruins of the Schrofenstein Castle perched on the forested flanks of the Brandwald - beautiful, picturesque places Bond knew well from before the war.

Past the village of Pfunds, split in two by the river…and then just 5 more kilometres to the Swiss border…

Soon after leaving the village, a little before the Kajetansbrücke, at a spot well out of sight of the village, Sonderhauser came to a stop. He got out of the VW, reconnoitred up ahead and, having confirmed there was no one around, he gestured to the others to join him. Bond and Jenkins switched to their boots, which they had been carrying in their knapsacks. They were, much better suited for hiking through the snow-covered mountains than their civilian shoes. Sabine was already wearing the boots she wore in the fields. They hoisted their knapsacks onto their backs, very light now, just containing a few supplies provided by Frau Sonderhauser - and a new bottle of schnapps in Bond's sack.

Sonderhauser removed a long, narrow case from the VW's boot. Opening it, he took out the three parts of a Greener double-barrelled shotgun, assembled them and handed the weapon to Bond along with a dozen shells.

'Take it, Andrew,' he said. 'I'm sure you won't need to use it, but it's better to have it, just in case!'

'Herr Sonderhauser, I don't want to take it from you,' Bond protested, knowing it was his favourite gun for hunting pheasants.

'Andrew, forget that nonsense! This is no time for niceties!' Sonderhauser snapped.

'I promise to return it to you after the war is over,' Bond told him, taking the weapon and pocketing the shells.

'Of course,' Sonderhauser said. 'Now, you remember the trail. You have a good five hours of daylight left. Even with the snow, you should be in Switzerland in a couple of hours…'

'I remember the way, Herr Sonderhauser.'

'Then off with you! Don't dally!' Sonderhauser snapped rather sternly, in an effort to hide his emotions.

They shook hands then Sonderhauser got back into the VW, turned it around and drove off.

Bond led the others along the road for a short distance until he found the trail that led up the mountain, staying on the north side of the river. This was why he had chosen this route. It led directly into Switzerland, hugging the mountainside, without having to cross any bridges over the Inn. The main road crossed the river at the Kajetansbrücke before reaching the border and the pass…much too risky.

The trail quickly started to climb upward through patches of untrodden snow in places, their boots leaving deep imprints in the surface. Where the sun had melted the snow, it left behind a glutinous mud in which their boots would get stuck, pulling free with an ugly "plop". A difficult hike, very different from the late springtime conditions under which he had walked this trail in the past with Sonderhauser as his guide.

A magical landscape, with shimmering snow-clad mountain tops around them, the tallest ones, barren crags reaching up sharply into the azure sky.

Bond kept up a quick pace, but not too relentless, to make sure Jenkins could keep up. As for Sabine, he had no doubts, she was in splendid physical condition.

Every so often, his senses constantly on the alert, he stopped whenever he had a clear view and surveyed the terrain around them. He couldn't afford to dismiss the possibility that there might be German patrols nearby. In that case, all they could do was hope to spot them first and hide, or find a way around them. Fortunately, the terrain here afforded many hiding places: rocky outcrops, scrub, dense pine forest.

At one point, as he was carefully making one of his frequent scans of the perimeter, he thought he saw something flash, like the sun reflected in a pair of field glasses. He allowed the others to go on ahead while he concentrated on the spot.

Nothing.

Snow, forest, mountains.

Absolute isolation, not the slightest movement.

Maybe he had imagined it. Maybe it was the sun reflecting off the ice. In any case, however, he was left with an uneasy feeling.

He passed the others and quickened his pace. Whatever it was that he had seen, the border was not far…

Oberscharführer Kurt Langer had chosen his observation post very carefully, in an outcropping of rocks on the side of the mountain. He had a good view of the river, the road to the border, the narrow valley of the Upper Inn, the slopes of the Glockturmkamm all the way up to its peaks and, from where he was, the mountainside that rose sharply up behind him to the craggy crest of the Blankakopf.

Further off, he could see as far as the tallest peaks of the Piz Mondin range that lay beyond the Swiss border.

Since receiving his orders a few days before, Langer and his three hand-picked men had been keeping watch at this spot. He concentrated his attention on the mountainsides knowing that there were trails there, even though they were mostly hidden beneath the snow. The road itself was covered by the border guard post. No fugitive would try to escape through there. If anyone were to attempt to cross into Switzerland from here, which he considered unlikely, it would have to be along one of those trails.

For three days, Langer and his men had been watching the same monotonous scene: the river, the road, the mountains – no movement, no one was heading toward Switzerland – the forests, the rocks, the snow with its dazzling whiteness that made the eyes ache, the cold despite the sun penetrating their heavy greatcoats since they were standing still most of the time. But orders were orders, no matter how absurd, and Langer had one of the virtues of a good soldier – patience. He would do whatever was ordered of him, for as long as it took, until his orders were changed.

He brought his field glasses to his eyes again, scanning the terrain slowly, carefully, leaving no spot unexamined.

Hold it! Over there! On the mountainside high above the road in a clearing in the forest. Three shapes trudging through the snow. He steadied his glasses and focused on the spot. No doubt about it, three figures moving along quite rapidly, as fast as the difficult terrain and the snow would permit, heading west along the trail.

Toward Switzerland.

Langer felt his heart beat faster in anticipation. This was how hunters felt when they finally glimpsed their prey. He had no doubts. Whoever the three were, they were fugitives. Their behaviour was at the least very suspicious and gave them away. If they weren't fugitives, they wouldn't be clambering up the mountainside heading for the border.

Langer lowered his glasses. In a voice tense with excitement, he ordered: 'Quick! Let's get moving!'

They left their hideout and ran down to the road where they had left their *Kübelwagen*. They drove as fast as they could to a spot on the road where a path led up into the mountainside. They jumped out of the vehicle.

Langer threw off his great coat, revealing his black SS uniform underneath. His men did the same. Making their way through the snow and brush with their long coats would only have been a hindrance – the day was getting hot and their exertions would keep warm them up.

They began to climb as quickly as they could. Langer could no longer see the fugitives but he estimated that they were about two kilometres ahead. He knew in which direction they were heading so he was sure that he would be able to catch up with them before they reached the border.

Bond still had that uneasy feeling warning him of danger. He stopped again, letting the others go ahead while he carefully studied the trail behind and below them. This time he could clearly make out four black figures silhouetted against the backdrop of white snow, climbing, almost running along the trail behind them. They had obviously spotted them and were now after them.

He caught up with Jenkins and Sabine, crying out, 'Let's get moving! We've been seen and they're after us!'

They picked up the pace for a while, almost running, but soon slowed down a little as Jenkins couldn't keep up such a fast pace on the snowy trail. At one point, Jenkins slipped on a patch of ice, stumbled and fell. But he quickly got back on his feet, his clothes covered in snow. Sabine held out her hand to help him. She pointed to his knapsack and Jenkins understood. Taking it off his back, he handed it to her and she slung it over her shoulder.

The trail stopped ascending and levelled off, snaking along the mountainside.

Bond constantly kept one eye on the trail behind them. At times, their pursuers were nowhere to be seen, hidden behind rocks or trees or bends in the trail as it twisted along the mountainside. But there was no way that the Germans could lose them. All they had to do was follow their tracks in the snow. At other times, he did spot them and saw they were gaining ground. They were young and fit, unlike Jenkins. But the border was very close. The race lay in the balance but they could still win it.

Soon the trail began to descend, leading down to the ravine which separated the two ridges and at the bottom of which flowed the

Schalkbach, a raging torrent swollen with the waters of the melting snows. This was what served as the border between the two countries.

They picked up the pace again and finally caught a glimpse of the Schalkbach below. Sweat drenched their foreheads and their clothing, their hot breath forming clouds in the cold air. Jenkins slipped again, sliding for more than a metre on his back before coming to a stop and struggling back on his feet. Sabine held out her hand again and he took it. With sure-footed steps, she supported him and helped guide him down the steep trail.

The four Germans were now in plain sight, even closer now. Their shouts ordering them to stop could now be heard clearly, shattering the silence, echoing in the mountains. They were only about 500 metres away, about the same distance that separated Bond and his companions from the raging stream.

A shot rang out, but the distance was still too great, even for a well-rested marksman, let alone for one out of breath from running. The crack echoed throughout the mountains.

Sabine and Jenkins broke out into a run, slipping and sliding, using each other for support to remain on their feet as they neared the stream, the border, freedom, and safety, with Bond right behind them, almost falling himself, holding the shotgun high to keep it off the snow.

Glancing behind him, he saw one of the Germans fall face first into the snow, then get up, trailing behind the others, brushing the snow off his rifle.

Just two hundred metres more to the torrent and the stone bridge that crossed it… they were going to make it!

Another shot was heard, like a last desperate cry by the Germans as they saw their prey slipping away.

Jenkins and Sabine crossed the bridge at a run, the raging torrent foaming and roaring in the riverbed beneath them. Bond followed, five metres behind them. At the end of the bridge, they passed a weathered sign that read "You are now entering Switzerland".

The trail began to climb again, this time up the slopes of the Piz Mundin, with its peak towering above them, timeless and forbidding.

They kept on going, still not feeling any sense of relief. Bond wanted them to reach a safe distance before allowing themselves to rest. The Germans could still shoot at them from the other bank as the three of them headed up the trail. They had to cover a distance of at least 500 metres to reach the safety of the forest, out of sight of the Germans.

Bond glanced behind him and froze.

The Germans had crossed the bridge as well and were following them across the border.

When Langer saw the sign, he barely paused before making his decision. A wooden sign was not about to interfere with his orders! They could still apprehend the fugitives, they had almost caught up with them and there was no one on the Swiss side to stop him. No one would find out about the border violation.

'Quick, make for the trees!' Bond yelled.

Jenkins and Sabine turned around and saw that the Germans were still after them and only 300 yards away. And it looked as if they were winning the race.

Jenkins was breathing heavily and in spite of all his effort and Sabine's support he couldn't sustain the pace. The Germans were gaining.

Two more shots rang out. Bond saw the snow fly into the air just inches from Jenkins' boot. They wouldn't make it to the tree line. The Germans' fire would stop them before then. Bond hurriedly looked around for cover. Over there! Twenty yards above them, just off the trail, a cluster of large boulders.

'Run to those rocks!' he yelled.

They heard him and scrambled up the mountainside above the path, sinking almost to their knees in the deep snow. They threw themselves behind the boulders, Bond following close behind. Several more shots rang out and a bullet struck a rock next to his head.

He risked another look. The Germans were spreading out, two on the trail with rifles at the ready, the other two climbing up the mountainside. Their plan was obvious: to encircle them.

The safety of the trees was just 100 yards away, but it may just as well have been on the other side of the Atlantic.

Bond weighed the situation. It seemed desperate. The Germans had them pinned down and once the other two were above them - that would be the end. They would either have to surrender or be shot where they stood.

Bond recalled C's last words: "Under no circumstances must you allow Jenkins to fall into the hands of the SS or Gestapo. Do you understand, Bond?" And in about one or two minutes that was exactly what was going to happen… Guardian or exterminating angel…

Bond raised the shotgun. It seemed unbearably heavy in his hands. He aimed it at Jenkins, two yards away, lying flat against the rocks. Thankfully, Sabine was on the other side and couldn't see.

He raised the gun, aiming at his head. Jenkins, sensing something, turned and looked at him.

Their eyes met. Bond saw first surprise, then understanding. With his expression, Jenkins was telling him to go ahead and do it.

Bond's finger found the first trigger, pressed it slightly...one slight tug and it would all be over.

He sat there, time suspended, frozen, a breath separating life and death. Suddenly the shotgun, as if on its own, shifted its aim away from Jenkins. 'The hell with it!' Bond said to himself. There were some things that he could not do, war or no war, orders or no orders!

He took another quick look from behind the cover of the boulders. The two Germans climbing up behind them were moving slowly through the deep snow.

'Paul,' he said without turning to look at him. 'I'm going to try to create a diversion. I'm going to start shooting. You run for the trees...okay?'

'Right, Andrew!'

'Sabine, you stay here. There's no reason for you to risk it...you can tell them we forced you to come along as a hostage.'

She didn't reply.

'Ready?' Bond asked.

Bond changed his position behind the boulders, moving toward the edge. He cautiously peered over them and saw the two Germans clambering up. Two hundred yards away, out of shotgun range. But his shots might make them slow down, make them go for cover until they figured out what sort of weapons he had.

Bond shot both barrels in quick succession, ducked out of sight and quickly reloaded.

One of the Germans fell on his back in the snow and remained motionless.

Jenkins and Sabine leapt from behind the cover of the rocks and made for the trees as fast as the snow would allow.

Bond immediately took another two shots at the remaining German who was still climbing up to get behind him. The German knelt down and fired a burst with his Schmeisser[72]. The two Germans still on the trail below fired their rifles as well. He heard Sabine cry out but he couldn't raise his head to see. Then he heard a gunshot that seemed to come from above him.

The bullet struck Langer in the forehead as he was kneeling, throwing him back, spread-eagled onto the snow, dead before his body could even sink into it.

Two more bursts of gunfire sounded, automatic gunfire. What on earth was going on? The two remaining Germans didn't have automatic weapons, only rifles…

With their leader dead and an invisible, unknown enemy with lethal firepower at large, the two Germans on the trail down below lost any desire for heroics and self-sacrifice. They had crossed the

---

[72] Schmeisser: One of the many automatic weapons (*MP, Maschinenpistole*) in the German arsenal. The Allies frequently referred to all German automatic weapons as Schmeisser, just as they used the term Spandau (the location of a production plant) for all German machine guns.

border illegally and if picked up by a Swiss patrol they had no excuses to offer.

They turned around and ran off back toward the torrent, the bridge and the Reich.

Bond felt his hands clutching the shotgun shaking from the tension. He took a deep breath and turned to look up behind him at the forest.

Jenkins and Sabine had almost reached the trees.

A figure clad in white emerged from behind the trees and beckoned to them.

Then he shouted down to Bond.

Still in a daze, it seemed to him that the voice he heard had spoken in English.

CHAPTER VIII

Living

When Bond reached the trees he was met by a man dressed all in white, white boots, white trousers and a white anorak with a hood covering his head. He was holding a Sten gun.[73]

'Professor Jenkins and Lieutenant Commander Bond, I presume,' he said. 'You are a week late for our appointment. And who is the young lady?'

'A friend who helped us,' Bond replied. 'I'm sorry for the delay. I didn't know we were going to be met by a welcoming committee…'

'Arranged by your boss.'

Behind him two more men dressed in white materialised out of the snow, as if the snow itself had come alive, transforming into living snowmen. One of them held a Lee-Enfield rifle[74] fitted with a telescope, the other a Sten.

'Sergeant Archer,' the first man introduced himself. 'And this is Corporal Comfort and Private Taylor, B Squadron, SAS.'

---

[73]   Sten: English automatic weapon, easy to use and reliable.

[74]   Lee Enfield .303: Standard issue rifle of the British Army in both world wars.

The two greeted them with brief nods.

'You've been out hunting, Commander?' Comfort asked, pointing at the shotgun.

'Hunting SS, but you beat me to it,' Bond replied.

'I timed my first shot with your second,' Comfort acknowledged.

Bond noticed Sabine's arm. She had a dark patch on her sleeve, just under the shoulder. Taylor followed Bond's gaze. He put down his Sten against a tree, went back to where they had stashed their knapsacks, white like their uniforms, opened his and came over to her.

'Miss, I'll have to rip your sleeve,' he said. He did this with two expert slashes of his knife and examined the wound. He wiped away the blood. It was a surface wound, a graze that was bleeding slightly but not deep. Taylor packed some snow on it, pressing against the gash to stop the bleeding.

'This will sting a bit, miss,' he said as he applied an antiseptic and then sprinkled some sulpha powder on the wound.

Sabine winced slightly but didn't utter a sound, looking into Bond's eyes. Taylor then applied a dressing.

They set off with Archer in the lead. Emerging from the forest, they followed a downhill trail and as the sun was setting, reached a dirt road where an automobile with snow chains was parked. Bond noticed the diplomatic licence plates.

'Borrowed from the embassy,' Archer informed him, noticing what he was looking at.

After the SAS men loaded their gear and Bond's shotgun in the boot, they all piled in.

By that time, the mountain peaks had turned rose-coloured from the last rays of the sun. They seemed less magisterial and forbidding, closer to the measure of men.

It was night by the time they arrived in Bern. They were met by a team from MI6 and the ambassador inside the British embassy compound.

The next two days were spent on procedural matters, Bond's debriefing, and the exchange of communications. Strictly speaking, the three of them had entered Switzerland illegally and should have been remanded to a Swiss detention centre. But this was a special case. The embassy supplied them with papers indicating they were employed by the embassy, for Sabine as well, at Bond's insistence and with C's approval. The Swiss authorities were willing to turn a blind eye in this instance. It was now evident who was going to win the war and even though a neutral country, Switzerland was preparing to start cashing in on some of the services it had provided during the war.

After those two days, Bond and Jenkins exchanged goodbyes.

'We'll be expecting you in Birmingham for dinner and breakfast.' Jenkins said. 'With very real coffee - and I think we might manage a Martini as well!'

They shook hands. Their eyes said much more. The brief moments up in the rocks above the Schalkbach and their shared secret would bind them together for a lifetime.

On the third day a signal arrived from C informing Bond that Professor Oliphant, at the recommendation of Jenkins, had put his name forward for a DSO.[75] "I refused on your behalf, Bond. You

---

[75] DSO: Distinguished Service Order, the penultimate British military medal, after the Victoria Cross.

understand that we cannot attract any attention to our activities with awards and such," he wrote. But he did congratulate him on his promotion to commander and granted him two weeks' leave. He also informed him that he had made arrangements for Sabine to be employed at the embassy in Bern as a translator for the duration of the war.

• • •

Bond raised the crystal wineglass and savoured another sip of the 1938 Château Lafite Rothschild. It was fabulous, as was the truffle consommé and the pheasant with the *foie-gras* ravioli, just as fabulous as the Hotel Beau Rivage and Geneva.

And even more so, Sabine.

They had spent their first morning in Geneva shopping, after Bond had exchanged his remaining *Reichsmarks* at a bank. Along with two months' backpay for the time spent on the mission that the embassy had advanced him, his wallet was full and he used it to buy himself a suit and everything that Sabine needed since she had brought nothing with her.

Her transformation was stunning. She was wearing a black evening dress with a plunging neckline, silk stockings and elegant black heels. She also had on a string of pearls, matching earrings and a gold ring, the only belongings she had taken with her from her home. She had fixed her hair that framed her face and neck, its lustrous tresses falling to her shoulders, shimmering bronze with gold highlights catching the light. Some eyeliner around the eyes, bright red lipstick on her lips and the country girl had been transformed into a stunning cosmopolitan beauty.

There were not many guests in the dining room of the Beau Rivage as visitors were rare on account of the war. The four men seated at a table nearby, probably bankers, could not hide their admiring glances.

'To your health, Sabine,' he said.

'My friends call me Biene.[76] And we are friends, aren't we, Andrew?' she replied, raising her glass.

'Friends and allies, Biene.'

It was a magical day for Sabine. After the deprivations, the blackouts, the fear of the past year in the Reich, free, neutral Switzerland with its shops full, the people carefree…the lights at night, reflected in the calm waters of the lake, the lit streets, the elegant shop windows…it was another world, like living in a dream.

She had drunk a little too much, not used to alcohol. Her cheeks had a rosy glow. She felt wonderful, liberated, more daring than ever.

'Andrew, I 'm beginning to fall in love with you,' she said, in English.

'I didn't know you spoke English.'

'I learned some in school. You don't know much about me, Andrew.'

'We have two weeks ahead of us for me to find out,' he said as he took her hand in his.

---

[76]   *Biene*: "Bee"

Sabine smiled. It was the first time he had seen her smile, her first smile in many months. It was the most beautiful sight Bond had seen in a long time.

After dinner, they strolled along the lake for a while before returning to their adjacent rooms at the hotel. He escorted her to her door.

She opened the door. Her hand found his and she pulled him inside.

'Tonight I don't want to be alone, Andrew.'

He followed her inside willingly.

They went out onto the balcony overlooking the lake, reflected lights shimmering on its calm surface. Spring had finally arrived in Geneva, the trees and the earth had turned green but the evenings were still cooled by the breezes off the snow-clad mountains in the distance. Sabine shivered and snuggled up against him.

He sought her lips, which opened up eagerly for him, as if they had been counting the days since that first kiss, that second night in her home.

They went back inside. Sabine broke away from his embrace and stood a few steps away from him.

'Wait, Andrew!'

She took off her dress, revealing her body, wearing only a black bra, slip, garter belt and stockings which emphasised the whiteness of her skin.

'Do I please you?' she asked with a teasing smile.

In reply, Bond came up to her and held her tightly in his embrace. His lips and warm breath caressed her ear, her neck, making her shiver again, and then her breasts as he released her bra.

They fell onto the bed together. Bond paused briefly to heighten the sense of anticipation, admiring her body and her breasts, gently heaving as she breathed.

A thought crossed his mind. How unexpectedly this mission was ending: with a beautiful German woman in a hotel in Geneva. But then again, the language of love was universal, it recognized no national frontiers. Her body, her breasts, eager for his touch and his kisses bore no sign that they were English, American, French or German. They belonged to a beautiful young woman, a very brave one, one that would be greatly needed after the war in order help the world and Germany become a beautiful and better place once again.

He pushed away all thoughts of the war. For now, it could wait. They had two weeks ahead of them to enjoy life.

Epilogue

I've tried to work in, as convincingly as possible, real events and personalities into the story to create as persuasive a picture of the war as I could, going so far in some places as to include details, such as the description of an actual downing of a Lancaster by a German ace.

I named my protagonist Andrew Bond in honour of Ian Fleming, whose work was an inspiration for my own espionage novels. In future Andrew Bond stories, I'll be covering more aspects of WWII, blending fact and fiction, including his encounters with his deadly archrival Benno, and many others.

Finally, I wish to thank Katia Bafouni for her work on the manuscript, M. Economou for his help with the preparatory research, and Helen and Vicki Politis for their help and for the translation.

Bibliography

- Brickhill, Paul (2004), **The Great Escape**, W. W. Norton

- Carroll, Tim (2004), **The Great Escape from *Stalag Luft III***, Pocket Books (Simon & Schuster)

- Green, William (1967), **Fighters, War Planes of the Second World War, Vol. I**, Doubleday

- Jentz, Tom (1993), **Kingtiger**, Osprey New Vanguard 1

- Lake, Jon (2002), **Lancaster Squadrons 1942-1943**, Osprey Combat Aircraft 31

- Longmate, Norman (1983), **The Bombers**, Hutchinson (Arrow Edition, 1988)

- Scutts, Jerry (1998), **German Night Fighter Aces of WW2**, Osprey Aircraft of the Aces 20